SUITCASE HEART

Short Stories

Cree Toner

This book belongs to so many people. My dad, who taught me to read when I was five years old and has encouraged my love for writing my entire life. My mum, for teaching me to look for good in everybody and to believe that everyone you meet has a story worth telling. My brothers, who endured hours of unnecessarily elaborate games of playing pretend. My friends, for reading and supporting and loving just about everything I've ever written. My teachers, especially Liska Jetchick, Paula Valcke, John Hindlay, Denise Cruz and John Bemrose, who have mentored and inspired and made me feel luckier than I can ever describe. Dolores Mulligan, for whom I wrote my first book; I wish you were here to see this. Eternal gratitude to each of you.

Snow in London

It doesn't ever snow in London- not properly anyway, the way it does at home- but I'd been in England less than three months when the entire country lost their minds over twenty-two inches of snow. I came to London four months after I graduated from university. I was afraid I would never go. I was afraid I would be one of those people whose entire life could be mapped across a 70-kilometre radius, the kind of person who stays in their hometown because at least there they are smart and important.

In London, I was living in a four-bedroom apartment with a gay, German couple, Elias and Otis, who made their own soaps in the kitchen, a South African man, Henry, who was always hosting elaborate dinner parties, and a woman named Petunia who suffered dreadfully from Ombrophobia- the fear of rain.

My boyfriend's first words when I told him about my new roommates: "Val. Babe. You're fucking kidding about these people." Todd was a business major who wore Brooks Brother suits to brunch. He called any man over the age of eleven 'sir' but all women under the age of seventy-five 'babe'. My friends all told me I was only sleeping with him because he was like my father, which I felt was disgusting, offensive, and ultimately true. We broke up before Thanksgiving.

My mother's first words when I told her about the roommates: "Just think of them as new material, darling. Inspiration. Muses." I went to school for journalism. My mother was an artist. I grew up eating cheese sandwiches in her studio in the basement. She wore denim overalls and didn't shave her legs and was the only mother I knew who let their kid paint their bedroom anytime they wanted. When her art wasn't selling, she worked at a call centre in town, and used to bring me to the office with her. I'd fall asleep beneath her desk with the stack of books she'd bought me from the Goodwill that week. We drove out to the Goodwill almost every Sunday afternoon when I was a kid. My mom looked for ugly pictures in beautiful frames and vases she could break up and do mosaics with and clothes we could rip apart and put in the costume bin. I looked almost exclusively for books. Doris, the lady with the lazy eye who always worked Sundays, used to bring over a little blue footstool from behind the counter for me. I would plunk the footstool down at the far end of the book section, and I'd work my way down from there. When I was eight, I read *Catcher in the Rye* and understand hardly any of it, but I threw my head back and laughed out loud when Holden Caulfield said the word sunuvabitch. I read books about the Cold War and self-help books for newly single men and cook books and books about sex and drugs and love and death. My mom was also the only mom I knew who let their kid read anything they wanted.

My first two weeks in London, it rained every day. I was eating toast at the dining room table when Elias came out of his bedroom. He was wearing a pair of blue briefs and nothing else. "Someone will have to get Petunia's groceries if the rain doesn't stop," he told me.

"I feel like by someone, you mean me."

Elias smelled of lye and oranges. "Otis and I went last week for her."

"What about Henry?"

"Henry only goes to the posh places. Petunia is not posh." He put air quotes around the word posh. "You can't make it seem like you're only going for her, though."

"I've just gone shopping yesterday. I would only be going for her."

"I know. But you can't say that. Otherwise, she'll get upset."

"I'm not being mean," I said, though I was, "but why doesn't' she move to California?"

When I told Todd about this, he was outraged. "How fuckin' DARE they, babe. Let the Petunia babe starve." When I told my mother about this, she was overcome with emotion. "Elias sounds so caring. Give him my contact, if you think of it, darling." My mother's idea of heaven contained an endless supply of paint, blended margaritas, and gay men.

And so, on my twelfth day in London, I stood outside Petunia's bedroom, knocking softly on her door. When it rained, Otis and Elias helped Petunia nail a black tablecloth over her window so that she couldn't see it. She had a white noise machine and a ceiling fan, both of which helped to drown out the noise. "Come in." She was sitting at her desk, a pair of headphones around her neck and a notebook beside her computer. Petunia was a transcriptionist.

"What are you working on today, Petunia?"

"Some crackpot Mormon sermon."

"Cool. I might be going out for groceries in a bit. Do you need anything?"

Petunia looked at me sideways like she was trying to figure out if I meant it. "What are you getting?" she asked.

I heard Todd's voice. *Now you're making up fake groceries for this babe, babe?* I heard my mother's. *Tell her you're getting chickpeas and tampons. She'll believe that.* "Chicken. Pasta. I need milk."

"You eat meat?"

Jesus Christ. "I only eat chickens 'because I think that as a species, they're sort of all assholes."

"Chickens have full colour vision, Valerie."

"Right. So. Did you want anything or…?"

"Yeah, alright, I'll make you up a list. Cheers. Shut the door on your way out, thanks love."

Elias and Otis were melting coconut oil on the stove as I slipped on my mom's old rain boots she had insisted I take with me. "I'm off, then."

"Stay dry, *hase.*" Elias was still wearing only the blue briefs but had added a pair of yellow safety gloves and thick goggles, suctioned tight around his eyes.

I came back from the grocery store cold, wet, and slightly pissed off. I ached for the simplicity of two subway lines, predictable weather, ugly skyscrapers. I left Petunia's groceries in bags on the kitchen counter, but when I saw Elias had wrapped up a bar of soap and left it outside my door, I went back and unpacked her things.

I was interning for free at a newspaper. I transcribed tapes for actual journalists, picked up coffees that cost more individually than what the company gave me a day for lunch, and organized office supplies. When I was a scrawny eleven-year-old, reading the Sunday Times and dreaming of a life in which I would be the one writing the stories that some other scrawny eleven-year-old read, this was not exactly what I had pictured.

I called my mother one day on my break. "When does it start to feel real?"

"When does what feel real, darling?"

I felt so childish when I answered her question with- "Being a grown-up?"

I could hear her smiling through the phone. "It doesn't. You just get more responsibilities and have to start pretending at it."

It rained for three more days and then on my fifteenth day in London, the sun came out. I helped Petunia take the nails out of the black tablecloth and we went for a drink. We told each other about our parents. Petunia was the youngest of six children. "My dad liked proper meals. Mum cooked for all six of us, breakfast, lunch and dinner. Never bought anything frozen, not even canned peas. She snapped one year at Christmas, I was about nine. Brought through the plate we always had the turkey on- great big china plate, it was my gran's. And instead of turkey, there was two dozen hotdogs, cut down the middle and filled with canned stuffing."

"What did you *do*?"

"Jesus, nothing. None of us said a word. Thought my dad was going to cry. But we just pretended it was normal. I was honestly worried my mum would kill anyone who mentioned it. What about you?"

"Not much, really. My parents split up when I was small. Dad's been married three times since my mom, my mom hasn't been with anyone else."

"No one?"

"I mean. She's *been with* people." Men with overgrown beards and souls my mother often said were 'too gentle for this world' came in and out of our lives like pebbles thrown into the ocean; they neither added to nor took away from the world my mother recreated for me once my father left. "But nobody seriously."

We walked back in the late afternoon, a little drunk, our arms looped around each other's waists like schoolgirls. Henry was making chicken liver mousse. We helped him stencil leaves onto place cards for the table. I kept insisting I could draw a better leaf free hand and eventually he put a hand on his hip and said, "You ladies have been helpful. Now please fuck off back to your rooms."

London felt marginally more like home every day.

***

The day of the snowstorm, I woke up to Otis banging on my door. He was standing in the hallway, bouncing on the balls of his feet.

"Otis. It is five in the morning. What. Do. You. Want?"

"Open your curtains."

I pulled my curtains back. In the yellow glow of the street lamps, fat flakes of snow were falling. Our front yard, which had been dry grass and a few sad looking shrubs when I went to sleep, was blanketed in snow.

"They've got snow in Germany, don't they?"

"Yes, Valerie," Otis said my name like it was a curse. "But I've lived here for nine years and so I haven't seen it really snow since then. Elias says it's going to go all day, too."

I clapped Otis' shoulder. "That's great. Honestly. I'm happy you're excited about this. It's quite cute, actually, but I've got to be up for work in an hour, so I'm going back to sleep."

I grew up in a small town in southwestern Ontario. Winters of my childhood were spent tobogganing at the park near our house. We used to make vanilla ice cream by pouring a can of condensed milk into a bowl of snow from the yard and my mom taught me to hollow out oranges, fill them with seeds, and tie them to the trees for the birds.

My phone went off when I was in that middle space between being asleep and awake. I answered groggily. The voice on the other end barked at me. "Mallory- offices closed today. Absolutely cannot be bothered with it."

"Who-" They had hung up. I was momentarily confused and then remember Lucinda, the tight-lipped woman who oversaw all the interns in my department, and who called me many names, none of which were my own.

I got out of bed and opened the curtains again. It looked like maybe two feet of snow had fallen.

Down the street, a man was standing dejectedly at the end of his driveway, staring at the back end of his car. He was holding a small garden spade. "Holy shit," I whispered.

Elias, Otis and Petunia were all in the kitchen. "I think I'm fine right now," Petunia was saying. "So long as it stays snow, I'm alright."

"They're saying it's been eighteen years since we've had this much." Otis was making eggs and cracked another one into the pan when he saw me.

"There's a man down the street who's trying to dig his car out with the same tool you'd use to dig up weeds," I offered. "Have you got a shovel we could lend him?"

Petunia laughed, slightly hysterically. "Valerie. Nobody in the entire country owns a shovel."

"Yeah. Well. The paper called and told me not to come in."

"I don't think anybody's working today."

Henry came into the kitchen then, his head low, hands stuck into the pockets of his dressing gown. "It's a disaster." He said. "An absolute disaster. Tonight's meant to be molecular gastronomy night. I've wasted half of last week's paycheque making fucking balsamic vinegar pearls."

Elias removed a fried egg from Otis' pan with a fork. He bit into the middle of it, yellow yolk dribbling out of his mouth. "There is only one thing for it. We must drink. I'm serious. Eat your eggs and we're going to the pub."

"If Mr. Next Door is trying to chisel his way out of the driveway-will the bars even be open?" I asked.

Elias stabbed a new fork into another egg and passed it like a skewer to Petunia. "Valerie, love. The entire city's shut down. The entire city will be at the pub."

Although it was early, I called my mom. I didn't know why, but I wanted to leave her a voicemail, tell her how hilarious the whole situation was. She answered, half asleep and panicked. "What is it, darling? Is everything alright? Have you been shot?"

"No, sorry, Mom. Everything's fine. We've had snow." I started laughing, realizing how ridiculous this must sound to her. "Most the United Kingdom's had in twenty years, apparently."

My mom was laughing now, too. "Oh, Val. That's lovely. Enjoy it. Have a lovely day, darling. I love you. Next time you call me in the middle of the night, please have been shot."

The five of us trudged down to the pub. Petunia was wearing four woolen sweaters because she couldn't find her winter jacket and didn't want to wear her raincoat in case it encouraged the snow to melt.

"I told you." Elias was triumphant when we got to the bar and there was barely a free space to breathe in.

Pieces of conversations floated around us like songs.

"My gran is meant to be having a corn removed on her foot today and they phoned her up and said no chance. Only essential surgeries today. Can you really believe it?"

"Meant to be flying to Ibiza this aft- every bloody flight cancelled at Heathrow."

"Entire underground shut down-"

"It'll cost us billions, all the lost working hours-"

"Not that I'm complaining, mind you, but-"

"Well, that's the Tories for you."

Elias ordered a round of beer and we sat at the only free table, right at the front of the bar by the door. Every time someone came in, banging their boots together, shaking the snow out of their gloves, we were hit with the cold. Someone put the news on and a bald man was saying somberly, "We are urging everyone to pull together and pool resources to get London through this difficult situation."

A man at the bar raised his glass up to the television. "Certainly pal," he shouted. "No fucking problem."

The entire pub clapped. Otis kissed Elias, Henry was laughing, Petunia clinked glasses with the woman at the table behind us. I thought about how funny it was that the more things happened, the less wonderful they often seemed- hearing your favourite song on the radio was always so much better than playing it on purpose.

We walked past the park on our way home. I had never seen so many children there at once. I closed my eyes for a moment, and all around I could hear them playing, laughing, arguing, their voices all mixing together, and it sounded like so many winter afternoons from my own childhood.

At home, we ate all of Henry's balsamic vinegar pearls and lit the candles Elias hadn't wrapped up, and for Petunia we prayed that the snow would stay forever. I was happy.

Bobcat

When the kids were still young enough to have baths together, Michael always brought the radio into the washroom and listened to Prime-Time Sports. It was his favourite radio program, the only one he always made a point of listening to. The kitchen was his wife's space- she liked the country station, had a stack of CD's on top of the microwave that she rotated through during the summer. Most of Michael's spaces were in-between and temporary- he left small, purposeful traces of himself everywhere without claiming anything as his own, and the weekly lugging of the radio from downstairs up to the bathroom was one of these traces.

Michael would plug the radio into the outlet above the toilet, and so, to the children, it always sounded like the voices were coming from the ceiling. Stephanie splashed water up the side of the tub and Dylan played with the little plastic cars that sunk to the bottom and the three of them would listen absently to Bob McCown talk about coaches he thought should be fired and players he thought were terrible and players he thought were stupendous.

Dylan started playing hockey the winter he was seven. Michael had been taking them to rinks in the city since they were babies, pushing them around the ice on little plastic chairs. Most Friday nights after supper they drove to North York and watched the junior team play. Stephanie loved hockey the way she loved black and white movies and postcards in boxes at second-hand stores- she found it vaguely romantic. Dylan was the one who hung jerseys on his bedroom wall and knew all the rookie records. The first season he played, his team won the league. The coach took them all to Pizza Hut after and the kids passed the trophy around the table like it was the Stanley Cup and to them, it might as well have been.

***

Stephanie and Deborah had been in the car for almost twelve hours when they hit the deer. Stephanie was sitting cross-legged in the passenger seat. Empty Tim Horton's cups were stacked inside one another in the cup holder. Deborah was driving. Stephanie had had her license for eight months and Deborah said maybe she could drive on the way home- "It's all highway, sweetheart. I know *you're* a good driver" (this was not necessarily true), "it's just everyone else I don't trust." Stephanie thought her mother was punishing her for wanting to go to university so far away- Lakehead was 1400 kilometers from home. If she went to school in the city, she could live with her parents and take the subway to class and keep working at the movie theatre and save money.

Stephanie flicked the radio on every so often- blare of static, sometimes a fuzzy voice- then turned it off. She watched her mother's hands tighten around the wheel every time she did this. Stephanie knew it was bothering her mother and she also knew her mother would probably not ask her to stop.

Dylan had a hockey tournament that weekend. Their team spent the first few weekends of September selling potato chips and chocolate bars in Dundas Square to fundraise for this tournament. They bought matching navy blue jackets with their numbers stitched onto the back. Dylan had called Deborah around lunch to let her know they'd won their first game. Deborah was asking Stephanie to call Dad and see how the afternoon had gone when Stephanie saw the deer. In the same instant that she saw it- illuminated by the weak, yellow glow of the headlights- the car hit it.

It ricocheted off the corner of the hood. Stephanie watched it flying but she didn't see it land. The car was spinning, and Stephanie yelled, "Was that a fucking deer?" and Deborah yelled back, "LANGUAGE, STEPHANIE." When they were still, Deborah reached over the mess of empty cups and grabbed her daughter's hand. "Are you okay? I didn't even see it until right before."

Stephanie opened her door. "Do you think we killed it?" she asked her mother. She remembered one summer when her neighbour's cat was hit by a car and Stephanie had to get the neighbour and tell her that her cat was lying on the side of the road. Stephanie's dad went with the neighbour to the vet and she and Dylan sat on the curb and waited and the two of them cried when Dad came home and told them the cat had been put to sleep.

Stephanie shone the light of her phone on the road. She circled around the car. The hood looked like an after shot from one of Dylan's video games. "It looks pretty bad, Mom."

Deborah rolled down her window. "We should call somebody," her mother said. Stephanie nodded. "Do you see it?"

"I don't want to look." Stephanie said.

Deborah got out and crossed the road. "It's here." Stephanie followed the sound of her mother's voice. She felt small.

"Is it dead?"

"I don't- I can't tell." Deborah stepped toward it, and it shifted, slightly.

Stephanie had only seen one deer before this in her life. It was on her Grade Three field trip to Black Creek Pioneer Village. Twenty-seven little bodies sat on wooden pews in a warm room and watched a woman in a brown bonnet knead dough on a large wooden paddle. After lunch, they went outside and played cat's cradle with yarn that made her wrists itch. They'd been walking to the barn that bordered the edges of a forest and there had been a deer standing there. One of the children noticed it and pointed and there were a few moments of stillness and then somebody screamed, and the deer ran.

***

Dylan was buying a hot dog at the stand across the street from the arena. He heard somewhere once that they made hot dogs with all the leftover parts of a pig and that if you ate more than fifteen a year, your chances of getting cancer increased by like, twenty percent. He considered this as he paid and scooped relish and hot peppers from their plastic containers. Some mustard dripped off the side of the bun and fell onto his shoe. It was early November and Dylan hypothesized that he had probably eaten fifteen hot dogs since October. He tried to figure out, mathematically, your chances of getting cancer if you'd been eating roughly fifteen hot dogs a month for six years, but it made him feel sick, so he stopped.

They had a few hours between games. Coach told them to stay close, drink chocolate milk for protein, and not be stupid. Some of the guys with girlfriends had snuck off, presumably to commit what Coach would consider the ultimate act of stupidity. Dylan had made out with precisely two girls in his life and he had found both experiences underwhelming. The first time, at a Canada Day party when he was fourteen, he got a surprise boner and had to spill his beer on the girl, so he had a way out before she noticed. The second time was the night after he got his braces off and he was having a hard time concentrating on the girl because his teeth felt so smooth. He kept accidentally running his tongue over his teeth and at first the girl thought it was a move, but then she just thought it was weird. It occurred to Dylan, at that exact moment, that maybe the experience of making out with girls was not underwhelming so much as he, Dylan, was an underwhelming person to make out with.

Dylan threw out his napkin and headed back to the arena. His father had gone home after the first game to let the dog out and do some paperwork. He had been gone for nearly two hours. Fleetingly, Dylan wondered if maybe his father was having an affair. He knew that was stupid and, furthermore, impossible. Earlier that day, Michael had sent their family group chat a photograph of the dog in the backyard and then another of the tuna melt he'd made for lunch. Michael was incapable of overtaking a car on the 401 without waving at the slow car to assure them there were no hard feelings about their lack of speed. Dylan didn't want his dad to be cheating on his mom, but it would have been sort of exciting. "My parents split up," he imagined himself saying somberly. "I am the product of a broken home." Maybe Harley Pisani from second period would feel sorry for him and she'd teach him how to enjoy kissing more.

A few of the moms from the team were sitting behind a folding table inside the arena. They were selling raffle tickets. He nodded at them as he walked past the table and turned down the hall toward the change room.

***

Michael was sitting cross legged on the kitchen floor, feeding his leftover tuna melt to Maggie. If Deborah was there, she would tell him he was going to make the dog fat. If Deborah was there, he probably would not have been eating a tuna melt from a paper towel while sitting on the floor.

They got Maggie from the OSCPA the first year the kids were old enough to really want something for Christmas. They told them that a dog was expensive, and Dylan offered to quit hockey for a year. They told them that a dog required a lot of work and walks throughout the day, and both kids offered to quit school indefinitely.

"In principle," Michael told his wife, as they walked past snouts pushed through chain link and high-pitched yelps, "I am against this." They bought the dog two days before Christmas and kept her at Deborah's mother's. On Christmas Eve, Deborah set her alarm for four a.m., so she could pick Maggie up and make coffee and put Maggie under the tree with the red bow she had bought from the dollar store. Deborah waited at the bottom of the stairs while Michael woke the kids up and when they came clumping down the stairs and saw the puppy, both of them cried for so long that Deborah worried maybe they were allergic.

Michael never liked dogs growing up. He hated that you'd find their hair on your black pants and he hated their drool and he hated the way they smelled. Michael had also never particularly liked children until he held his daughter for the first time. Michael did not like dogs and he did not like children, but he loved his own dog and children like they were the perfect Platonic prototype of Dog and Children.

Maggie nudged his knee with her nose. "It's gone." He showed her the empty paper towel, then he showed her the other side, so she would know he was being truthful. Maggie rolled over on her side, her spine curving away from Michael. "I'm sorry," he told her. He got up off the kitchen floor and opened the cupboard above the sink and took out the yellow plastic bag that they kept her treats in. He shook the bag and the dog rolled back over and trotted over to him.

When Stephanie was young, her favourite thing to eat was a toasted tomato sandwich with a pickle on the side. When she was nine, she fell off the monkey bars at school and broke her left arm. After they came home from the hospital and Deborah tucked her into the couch and put on cartoons, Michael went into the kitchen and toasted two slices of bread. He cut the tomato and made sure the pickle wasn't touching the crusts of the sandwich. He brought it into the living room and Stephanie smiled softly and said, "Daddy, I only liked this when I was little." Michael's favourite thing about his children was watching them grow into people, watching as they learned to make jokes, making mental notes when things they love became things they loved. Michael's favourite thing about Maggie was that every time they he gave her a treat, it was exactly what she wanted.

He let Maggie out once more, waited while she peed on the side of the fence, locked the door, and got in the car to drive back to the arena.

***

Over her mother's pleas that it might be diseased or rabid, Stephanie was sitting on the shoulder of the road with the deer's head in her lap. Deborah had tried calling the police but couldn't get service. She told Stephanie that they had to get in the car and drive to the next town. "It's dying, Mom. We can't just leave."

Deborah liked happy endings to the point where she would not watch a movie unless she had a full guarantee it didn't end sadly. Whenever she heard about a missing child on the news, she would always wait a few hours and then go on her computer and look up the child's name. Most times, they had been found and were back at home. It comforted Deborah to know that all she had to do was wait and a child could go from missing to found. She didn't want to stand in the dark, on the edge of a quiet road, somewhere in between Toronto and Thunder Bay and wait for this animal to die.

"Can you get my sweater from the car?" Stephanie asked.

"Ten more minutes, Steph, then we're leaving." Deborah said. "I'm putting the radio on," she called out from across the road, the dark swallowing her voice. "It's too quiet." Stephanie's sweater tucked under her arm, Deborah turned the keys in the ignition. She stood in between the door and the driver's seat, trying to find a station.

Stephanie pet the top of the deer's head. "It's okay," she said. Its eyes would flutter closed for a few moments, and then open again. It reminded her of Jordan, the little boy she babysat, when he was trying to fight a nap.

The only channel Deborah could find that wasn't white noise was the sound of a man's voice. He was speaking to a woman. "Now you see," he was saying to the woman, "that's where you're wrong." The voice crackled a little and cut out, but then came back. She turned it up so that they would hear it from the other side of the road. She draped the sweater over her daughter's shoulder and kissed the top of her head.

The sound of the couple's voices drifted from the car over to Stephanie and her mother, "It's just not possible," he said. "If you look at last year's season and that trade, you'd see that Davidson was much stronger on-"

Stephanie tilted her head back, careful not to disturb the deer. "Hey. I think that's that guy. That sports guy. The one we always listened to with Dad."

They were both quiet for a moment. Deborah smiled. "Bob McCown."

"Yeah." She remembered sitting across from her brother in the bathtub, rainbow speckled bubbles that webbed her fingers together and the green cup her dad would use to rinse their hair. She was two years older than her brother, but when she watched him playing hockey, she always felt like she was his little sister. She couldn't have said why, but she felt like crying.

Stephanie sat with the deer for another half hour before it died. Once she made sure it had stopped breathing, she pressed her lips to the tips of her index and middle finger and then placed her fingers lightly on the deer's nose. "Okay?" Deborah asked. "Okay," she said, wiping her hands on the side of her jeans as she stood up.

***

A few of the boys from the team were already in the change room when Dylan got there. "It smells like shit in

24

here," Dylan said, by way of greeting.

"Your mom eats shit," Mark, their goalie, said. Mark coughed. "Sorry. I didn't mean that. Your mom's a nice lady." Dylan unzipped his equipment bag, took out one of his socks and threw it at Mark.

The change room door opened, and Coach came in. Coach was carrying a Styrofoam cup of coffee, and a Diet Coke. When Dylan was younger, he and Michael used to practice taking slap shots in front of the house every night after Michael came home from work. Dylan had this old hockey net, the red coating rusted from being left out when it rained. Michael recorded games for Dylan on school nights, and the next day they would sit down and watch them together. In an abstract way, they sometimes talked about Dylan going to college in the United States on a hockey scholarship. Dylan probably wasn't good enough to get a full ride (or even a half ride) and he was pretty sure they both knew it, it was mostly just fun to imagine.

Mark and the rest of the guys left the change room to get food. They invited Dylan, but the weight of the hot dogs and his impending cancer diagnosis were pulsing in his stomach, so he declined. Coach was the only one left. Dylan started cleaning his skates for something to do. "You mind if I put this on?" Coach asked him, gesturing to his phone. Coach was gruff and last week he called Dylan a pussy twice in practice, but he was thoughtful in very particular ways. Dylan's grandmother died last Christmas, and Coach came to the funeral alone and stood in the procession line for half an hour just so he could clap Dylan's hand and awkwardly hug Deborah.

"Go ahead," Dylan said, rubbing a patch of dirt out of the right boot.

A lull of silence, and then a man's voice, slightly distorted from the echo, filled the change room. "Now you see, that's where you're wrong." The man said.

"Hey," Dylan said.

The man was talking to somebody else. He sounded annoyed but also like he was enjoying himself. "It's just not possible," he was saying. "If you look at last year's season and that trade, you'd see that Davidson was much stronger on-"

"I know that guy."

"Bob McCown?" Coach asked. "Of course, you know the fuckin' Bobcat."

Dylan laughed, quietly, surprised that he was laughing even as he was doing it. He learned to skate before his third birthday, but his first real introduction to hockey, to its beautiful intricacies and how it could make him feel, was on those nights in the bathtub, his whole world and that radio in their tiny bathroom. He went back to cleaning his skates.

***

Michael was driving back to the hockey arena. He remembered the summer they took the kids to Nova Scotia. They'd taken out the fifth Harry Potter on audiobook from the library and packed the backseat with boxes of granola bars and trail mix and peanut butter sandwiches. Dylan and Stephanie counted how many dead animals they saw and how many people they could get to wave at them and how many cars on the 401 looked like theirs. The drive had been seventeen hours- only a hundred and twenty minutes longer than the drive from home to Thunder Bay. Michael used this to try and make Deborah feel better about the possibility of Stephanie being at school there. "We're losing her," Deborah said to Michael back in September, after the university fair at Stephanie's high school. "We can never lose her completely." He told her. "She'll always be our daughter."

He said these things to Deborah, but he didn't know the fullness with which he believed them. What was the word for not understanding the depth of your parents' affection for you until you yourself were a parent? The lack of believing it was possible to feel that much- too much, sometimes.

After Stephanie was born, Michael walked up and down the halls of the hospital with her, talking to her. He couldn't think now what he had said to her then, but he had a distinct memory of telling himself to remember every corner of this moment. After Dylan was born, Michael called his parents from a payphone in the waiting room, his hands shaking as he pushed quarters into the slot, the words "I have a son" bursting from him like a bullet.

Michael indicated left and switched the radio on. He'd taken Stephanie driving the other night and he let her pick the music if she agreed to keep the volume on low. A girl was singing, her voice upbeat and slightly twangy against a low thudding bassline. He changed the station.

"Now you see, that's where you're wrong," Bob McCown's voice, so familiar that Michael sometimes felt he actually knew the man to whom the voice belonged.

When the kids were small, Deborah kept a book of all their firsts- Stephanie's first word was duck, a Ziploc bag held a curl from Dylan's first haircut. He couldn't remember when the last first was- the last thing their children had done which they deemed to be the first of its kind. It was funny how almost every child that ever grows does almost identical things which almost every parent believes to be unique. He wondered about the last time he had unplugged the radio, carried it upstairs, knelt on the other side of the white bath tub and washed his children's hair.

"It's just not possible," Bob McCown said. "If you look at last year's season and that trade you'd see that Davidson was much stronger on -"

Michael turned into the parking lot of the hockey arena. He sat for a moment, enjoying this in-between space, before he turned the car off and opened his door.

Backward and Forward

Yeva Thanatos was born a bookend. Her father, Ciaran, whispered this into the damp crown of her head when she was only moments old and every year on her birthday, her mother, Esther, made a lemon cake into which she baked the entirety of her daughter's life. Ciaran and Esther's only child had a first name which meant life and a last name which meant death. Ciaran's father came to this country when he was seventeen, with his wife, who carried inside her the first member of the Thanatos family that would not be born in the old country. They were welcomed to America by a green woman who wore a crown, a small man who wore a crumpled suit, and the beginnings of Ciaran's mother's labour pains.

Yeva Thanatos spent the first sixteen years of her life sharing a bedroom with the woman from whom her father had come. Yeva's paternal grandmother changed her name from Nechama to Margaret the same day that she gave birth to Yeva's father. She had not been in America for twelve hours, but she had been on that boat for what felt like twelve years and as soon as her feet were on solid ground, she wanted to forget everything that had been. Lying labouring in the back room of the house the man with the crumpled suit took them to, Nechama-who-would-become-Margaret was becoming a tree. Her feet: toes curled in pain into the white bed-sheets, the lines on her soles mapped her life like growth rings on a tree trunk, her father told her once that if you counted all those rings you'd know the tree like you knew your own hands. Her hands: the opal engagement ring Avi bought her, tight around her swollen finger, the palms of her hands opening and closing like roots fighting their way down through soil.

Towards the end of Margaret's life, she began to live backwards.
In February, she thought it was December of that past year. She
began to speak about Avi, Yeva's grandfather who had passed
away when Yeva was four weeks old. "He should be back soon,"
Margaret said to Yeva one evening. "He's just gone to get milk."

In the last six months of her life, she would answer only to
Nechama. One day in early October, a letter came in the mail
from the bridge club that Margaret belonged to. Yeva was eating
Oreos on her bed when her grandmother opened the letter.
Margaret sat down beside Yeva and pointed to the typed words at
the top of the sheet. "Margaret." She put her teeth together and
clucked her tongue. "Who is Margaret?"

Yeva twisted apart an Oreo. "*You're* Margaret, Bubbe."

Margaret made a sound like she was going to spit. Later on,
doing the supper dishes, Yeva asked Esther if her grandmother
really didn't know who she was. "She knows who she is. She's
just confused." Esther pushed up the sleeves of her shirt and
dunked a wine glass into the soapy water.

Yeva didn't think her grandmother was confused. On the front
page of the paper last week was a photograph of the only mosque
in town. Somebody, or some bodies, had spray painted a red
swastika on the side of the mosque and kicked over the daffodils
that had just started to bloom in the front garden. Margaret was
staring at the paper when Yeva came home from school. Yeva
got the same feeling in her stomach that she had at Uncle
Daniel's funeral, when she'd seen her father cry for the first
time.

Another thing of the past to which Nechama began to cling was
picking Yeva up from school. This was something she had done
every day when Yeva was young. Esther and Ciaran both worked
in the city and were usually not home until after dinner. Nechama
used to drive a neon Ford Fiesta. She was perpetually "freezing

to death" and believed everybody else was as well, and so she left the house forty minutes early for the fifteen-minute drive to Yeva's school. She did this to let the car warm up for her granddaughter. Nechama kept a bag of chocolate covered raisins in the glove compartment because they were Yeva's favourite. The chocolate was often soft and sticky on Yeva's fingers.

"Tell me all of it, bubbale." This was how Nechama always began their car ride conversations. Yeva would open the passenger door (her grandmother didn't believe that children should sit in the backseat), greeted by a blast of hot air and those familiar words.

When Yeva started fifth grade, she decided she was old enough to take the bus home. Esther was packing her lunch and when she said, "Bubbe will get you tomorrow, yeah?", Yeva's stomach turned. She'd been rehearsing this moment since July.

"Charlie started taking the bus last year and we were talking, and she said she takes one that practically comes right to our house." Yeva was standing behind her mother. Esther had her back to her daughter.

Esther was quiet for a moment. Inside her head, there was a war waging. She wanted her daughter to stay small and dependent on them forever. She wanted her daughter to grow up braver and stronger than she had. She wanted her mother-in-law to feel like Yeva needed her. She wanted her mother-in-law to not need to feel needed. "Okay, sweetheart. I'll have to call Charlie's mom and talk to her about it. But that should be okay."

That same year, Yeva also decided she was too old for her father to pick her up on her birthday. After she was born, while her mother was in the shower, Ciaran had held his infant daughter in his hands and walked with her up and down the hallway of the hospital. He wove strands from his life into her tiny, perfect, pink ears and told her the story of her birth and what little life she had lived thus far. For the next ten years, Ciaran would hold his daughter in his arms on her birthday and walk with her around the house. This was as natural to Yeva as the fact that she had a birthday at all. On her eleventh birthday, Yeva was in her bedroom with her friends. They were painting each other's nails when Ciaran knocked on the door. "Mama and I are going out to get the pizzas, do you want to do the walk now or after we eat?" Yeva curled her hands into balls, smudging her nail polish. She shook her head. Ciaran hesitated. "Oh." He waited a moment and then Yeva sunk back into her bedroom.

The older she got, and the more distance that grew between her and those memories, the more she hated the eleven-year-old who sent her father and grandmother away. The older she got, the more she came to understand a fraction of the pain that comes with losing the people you love, piece by piece.

Five months before Nechama died, and one month after she stopped answering to Margaret, Yeva's grandmother left the house an hour before the high school let out, and got on the bus. She sold the neon Ford Fiesta last May, when she'd pressed the gas instead of the breaks at a red light. She'd gone to pick up cigarettes late in the evening, so no one was around to know it had happened, but it frightened her so much that she told Ciaran to get rid of the car the next day.

Yeva came out the front doors of her school and saw her grandmother sitting on the bench where everyone usually smoked. A tall, thin boy was sitting awkwardly at the other end of the bench, a cigarette between his thumb and index finger. Yeva stood at the top of the school stairs and watched her grandmother. "Bubbe," she called out to her. Nechama turned and raised her hand.

When Yeva approached the bench, Nechama stood up. "Filthy habit," she said conversationally to the boy smoking.

"Bubbe- what are you doing here? How did you get here?" Nechama looped her arm through Yeva's.

"Home is boring. Nobody to talk to. I missed you. I got on the bus. Easy. Idiot could do it."

"What about bridge?"

Nechama joined the bridge club after her husband died. She went twice a week to the seniors centre, with a travel mug of gin and a freezer bag of homemade sugar cookies. She complained mercilessly about belonging to a bridge club. She said bridge was for miserable old ladies who had nothing left to live for and lonely old men who were hoping one of the miserable old ladies would fall asleep and let themselves be fondled. Yet, she had a near perfect attendance record and when Yeva went with her father to pick Nechama up after the game finished, they often sat in the car a half hour later than they'd planned to because she wasn't ready to leave.

Nechama made the spitting noise again. "That place makes me feel like my teeth are going to fall out." Nechama stopped to pull up the collar of her coat. "Anyway, bubbale. Tell me."

"Do you want to get milkshakes, Bubbe?"

Nechama's eyes shone like a child's. "Could we? What about dinner?"

The first time Yeva could remember going to play at somebody else's house, she asked her friend, "Where's your grandmother?" when they went into the girl's bedroom and there was only one bed and no blue pill case with the days of the week on it or a thick stack of Reader's Digests on the floor. Nights when Yeva was young and couldn't sleep, she would crawl into bed beside Nechama. Nechama, half asleep, would turn on her bedside lamp and she and Yeva would do the crosswords together. *Grocery container. Spherical hairstyle. Auction conclusions?*

Yeva squeezed Nechama's hand. "We'll be backwards, today."

They walked to a diner that Yeva and her friends often went to after school. The waitresses were all middle-aged women who wore bright lipstick and never wrote down what you ordered. They served breakfast all day and the milkshakes came in fountain shoppe glasses with whipped cream and a maraschino cherry. You could see them mixing the shakes up behind the counter. Yeva ordered them each a chocolate milkshake and a stack of pancakes to share.

When the waitress brought them their food, Nechama gestured at the woman and said to Yeva, "*Yeshua,* did you see the tits on her?" Yeva laughed so hard that whipped cream came out her nose.

"Bubbe, you can't *say* those kinds of things." She said once she'd stopped laughing.

"Sure, I can. It was a compliment. Yours are small, like mine. Little peas. Not good for babies."

"Well. I think I've got some time before that becomes a huge problem for me."

Nechama reached across the table and patted Yeva's hand. "Good girl. Legs crossed."

Once they'd eaten, Yeva paid and they went outside to wait for the bus. Nechama sat by the window and stared through the dirty glass for most of the ride. She pointed out a rabbit that was hiding underneath a bush and waved at a group of school children. Yeva wondered if her grandmother recognized herself in these children the way that, in spite of her being seventeen, Yeva still did.

When they got home, Esther's car was in the driveway. She met them at the door. "Nechama, I was so worried about you." Esther was still trying to navigate how to treat her husband's mother in the wake of her encroaching senility. She treated Nechama too much like a child, and felt like a bully, or else she treated her the way she always had and felt negligent.

"I got Yeva from school." Nechama said, as if it wasn't six years since she had last done this.

Esther looked at her daughter and Yeva nodded. "We had fun," she told her mother and was surprised to find she meant it.

Almost every day for the next three months, Nechama took the bus to pick up Yeva from school. Esther made her take one of their spare cellphones so she could track Nechama's location from work. Periodically, Ciaran would say to his daughter, "You don't have to keep doing it. If it's too much, she can just stay at home." Part of Yeva wanted that, though she felt shame when she allowed herself to acknowledge it. A part of her flared up with embarrassment when she came out of school and saw her grandmother sitting on that bench, surrounded by a bunch of teenagers with leather jackets and cigarettes. But an equal, if not bigger, part of her felt these afternoons with Nechama were like the moments she had spent as a child, sitting cross legged on the dining room floor, trying to cup the rainbow from her parents' crystal sun catcher in her hands: fleeting and special and even though she wasn't sure what the point was, she didn't want to stop.

Yeva couldn't remember the exact moment she stopped telling her grandmother everything. She used to wake up in the night and tiptoe across the carpet, her small body a giant shadow in the light of the moon. She used to crawl into bed with her grandmother and wrap her own legs around Nechama's and whisper her dreams into her grandmother's ears. If she was sick or sad or scared, she went to her grandmother before she went to either of her parents. Charlie used to ask her, "How do you stand that?" when she slept over at Yeva's and Nechama was snoring and Yeva would want to ask her the same thing when they slept at Charlie's and her bedroom was silent.

These afternoons didn't bring that closeness all the way back, but it felt nearer to Yeva than it had in years. Cautiously, Yeva started to ask for stories about her grandmother's life. She was

worried both about hearing too much and not enough.
Nechama told her granddaughter about the Polish family that lived across the street from her and Avi when they first moved to America and how she used to give their little boy a strip of raw bacon before he went to school. She told Yeva that her first memory was sitting on her own mother's lap, hands cupped under her mother's as she showed her how to form shredded potatoes into a pancake shape for latkes.

One afternoon, they got caught in a thunderstorm walking to the diner. Their coats hung on the outside of their booth, dripping water onto the floor. One of the waitresses- most of them knew Yeva and her grandmother by then- brought a faded yellow towel for Nechama to put around her shoulders. That day, Yeva asked for the story of how Nechama met Avi.

"We were at a dance," Nechama said, her hands wrapped around a white mug of hot chocolate. "I was with Leah. Beautiful girl. Boys always loved Leah. Avi came over and I say to myself, oh here we go. Another boy who loves Leah. I am thinking this in my head and then it is quiet, and I realize he is asking me to dance." She told her that Avi taught her to read English by himself and that he made the best coffee in the world and that he loved to dance but had two left feet.

When she was small, and her parents went away for the weekend, Yeva and her grandmother had what Nechama called backwards days. They woke up and put their pyjamas on. For breakfast, Nechama made Yeva's favourite dinner- macaroni and cheese from the box. They spent most of their mornings lying on the couch together. They played a game where they had to take turns making up words and deciding what they meant. (*Tupress:* the feeling of being squished tightly in-between two business men on the L Train. *Winooze:* when you think you're going to sneeze and spend a few moments with your face all scrunched up but then the sneeze goes away, and you're left feeling sort of stupid and dissatisfied. *Yimello:* when you leave Jell-O in the fridge for too long and the top layer gets hard and gross.) For dinner, they had pancakes and fluffy scrambled eggs. After, they put on fancy clothes from the dress-up box and walked around the house with books on their heads to help their posture. They slept in her parents' bed on these weekends, and Yeva often fell asleep in the dress up clothes, swimming in the sleeves of her father's old suit jackets and her mother's discarded pearls.

Towards the end, although Yeva did not know it was towards the end, they started playing the imaginary word game again. They went to go see a movie, and in the theatre, the lights dim, a tub of popcorn balanced on the armrest between them, Nechama leaned over and said, "*Glozzom:* when you fart in a crowded room and pray to *Yeshua* that it's silent."

"*Chaka:* biting into a piece of popcorn that has way too much butter on it."

Nechama nodded. "Disgusting," she agreed. Nechama reached over and held Yeva's hand. When Yeva got to be around the age that she started believing she was outgrowing her family, she hated when Nechama held her hand. Walking to get lunch or to go temple, Nechama would hold Yeva's hand, her fingers warm and soft. Yeva used to silently count to a hundred and then take her hand back, pretending she had an itch, putting her hand in her pocket, taking her phone out. In the movie theatre, Yeva squeezed her grandmother's hand, and held back.

***

  Nechama died in the exact opposite way that she lived: alone, with very little noise or fanfare. She had a massive heart attack. Esther came home after lunch and found her.

Two weeks before her heart attack, Nechama told Yeva that after Avi had died, Nechama came to stay with her son for what was intended to be a few weeks. Esther thought it might help Nechama to have another body near her own, so they moved Yeva's crib from their bedroom into the spare room.

"I was so lonely." Nechama said. She was sucking the leftover whipped cream out of her milkshake, but she was staring out the window and her eyes looked like she was faraway. "You can't imagine, bubbale. What it is like to love the same person for so long, to do everything with them, and then they are gone. Like someone ripping you apart."

After they took Nechama to the morgue, Yeva went up to bed. She was lying with her back turned away from where Nechama had slept when Esther opened her daughter's bedroom door. Her husband was downstairs, calling the cousins. Esther got into bed with Yeva.

With her eyes still closed, Yeva told her mother what Nechama had said about Avi. "It *was* only going to be a few weeks," Esther laughed. She wound a curl of her daughter's thick, brown hair around her index finger, and held it there. "You were such a fussy baby. You cried every night after we brought you home. All night. For four weeks. Once, I took you out onto the balcony and I remember thinking, 'If I dropped her, she'd stop crying.'"

Yeva laughed. "That's a nice thing to hear your own mother say."

"I would never have done it. I just thought it. Anyway. That morning, we woke up and you hadn't cried at all. Papa got up to check and he came back to get me and-" Esther's voice broke a little, she swallowed, this moment needed to be for her daughter, "your grandmother was sleeping sitting up in bed and you were curled up, asleep, this tiny ball in her arms. I remember just looking at your little fingers wound up in hers."

Yeva's eyes were still shut, but there were tears leaking out of them, running sideways across her nose and falling onto the pillowcase. "I didn't know that."

Esther let go of her daughter's curl and squeezed her shoulder.

They lay like that, side by side, not speaking, arms overlapping, until they both fell asleep.

Mouse

The spring I was eleven, my mother woke my sister and I and said, "We are going to hike in a straight line" and we left the house. I remember I had the backpack my grandmother gave me. It was blue with lopsided straps and a pouch in the front where I kept things that were special and also small.

I learned to speak English by watching the television in the stuffy living room of the house we went to while my mother cleaned the washrooms at the hospital. The woman who lived there kept the blinds drawn and for lunch she warmed hot-dogs in the microwave. We ate them off thin, damp paper towels. From the other children, I remember runny noses and small, sweating hands and cheeks imprinted with the lines from the leather couch where we often fell asleep in the afternoon. From home, which Mother and Marta and I left the winter I was seven, I remember a man who was my father teaching me how to peel potatoes, his gruff hands gentle around my small wrists, a waste basket where I put the skins and a wooden cutting board where Mother diced the potatoes. I remember watching Mother fold white linen napkins into squares small enough to fit in the bottoms of wicker Easter baskets, Marta and I fighting over who got to carry the basket to church, the itchy nylon tights I tore a hole through playing in the parking lot after service.

We were each allowed to bring a bottle of water and one thing to eat; Marta chose a plastic package of gummy fruit snacks and I chose an apple. It was the kind of day where you couldn't tell if it would rain or not. The sky was grey on one half of the town and there was a warm breeze that seemed to carry the word 'soon' on its back.

We lived on the hill behind the golf club. People used to get upset that our house was where it was. Retired men with skin like leather paid good money to play golf at the club and we had the nerve to live there. Our house *did* look out of place. It was built early, dropped down on top of the hill like a mistake, built before the other houses, houses with swimming pools and big backyards. Our house had a yellow door and a kitchen sink tap that dripped all night unless you turned the tap all the way to the left. Marta and I shared a bedroom. We had a pink carpet that split our room in half and matching wooden night tables. Once, when we were young, Marta dragged a spool of thread around her half of the room and said I wasn't allowed to touch anything inside the thread. I annoyed her by lying on the floor and waving my hands back and forth so that the thread moved marginally closer to me.

We left the house in a line- Mother, then Marta, then me. Marta is two years older than me. That spring, she wore a white training bra and kept a box of tampons in her bedside table, but if we wedged the desk chair under our doorknob, she would still play dolls with me.

Mother didn't check to make sure the door was locked before we left, so I checked twice. "Aurelia," Mother said. She secretly hated when I got nervous. She took us swimming once at the recreation centre. She bought matching purple two pieces with frills around the bottoms for Marta and me. She wore a black one piece because she didn't like people looking at her body. She said her stomach had too much fat, but at home the three of us took baths together and I thought she was beautiful. The pool had a blue diving board. You had to climb up a metal ladder, then step out onto a tiny square platform before you walked out onto the board. Marta went first, and I watched the diving board bounce underneath her feet. She plugged her nose and jumped, legs straight and feet pointed down, toes curling as she fell. Mother was standing at the edge of the pool with her camera and when

41

Marta hit the water, she tucked the camera under her arm and clapped her hands. The handle of the ladder was slippery underneath my palms and when I put my foot onto the board, I knew I couldn't do it.

"*Myszko*, go on" I heard my mother calling, trying to coax me out onto the board. Marta was splashing underneath me. I shook my head and started climbing backwards down the ladder. The little boy behind me had to climb back down, too and he called me a baby. Mother said it was alright, maybe next year, but she held me hand a little too tightly when we were leaving, and I knew she was upset.

We walked straight across the grass of the golf club. The golf club closed at the end of last summer. One of Mother's friends from work said it was because the owner's money went to his nose. I thought this was the same as something going to your head, but the friend told us it meant that the owner was addicted to cocaine. Some of the grass was yellow and dry and the trees all had branches that were being pulled toward the ground. We walked past the back of the club. Somebody had broken one of the windows and you could see the cork-top tables in the dining room, naked without their tablecloths. When she wasn't cleaning houses, Mother used to help out at the club after weddings or christenings. If we promised to behave, she would take my sister and I. Marta and I would sit on swiveling leather stools and eat leftover roast beef sandwiches while Mother took down streamers and mopped up spilled beer.

Marta turned around, her brown eyes meeting mine, and I wondered if she was thinking about those nights, too. The both of us used to get dressed up whenever Mother got a shift at the club. I had a pair of black patent leather shoes with little pink ribbons on the heel and Marta wore the navy-blue dress with puffy sleeves and glitter on the top that the neighbour gave her when her own daughter outgrew it. Both items were too small, but they were our best clothes. We wore them so that we would look like we belonged to the club, instead of looking like we belonged to the immigrant woman stripping the tables.

I was aware, often painfully, of the fact that we were Not From Here, but I never blamed Mother for this. I never felt ashamed if we were out somewhere and her mouth was too fast for her brain and she slipped back to the language she had spent her first twenty-eight years speaking.

When Marta brought a friend home from school for the first time, Mother spent the afternoon cooking. She made *golbaki* for supper and *babka* for dessert. She laid our good plates out on the table. Marta's friend took one look at the *golbaki*, crossed her arms and said, "I'm not touching that." Marta was upset and told me later that Mother should have known to just make hamburgers. I ate the leftover food and told Mother that Marta's friend was a twat. I didn't know what the word meant, but I heard it on the television and it seemed to carry a weight heavy enough for a girl who wouldn't eat my mother's cooking. A laugh burst from Mother and then gently she tapped my cheek. "Bad word, *myszko.*" she said, but her eyes were shining. Mother secretly loved when I said things I shouldn't.

"It is a beautiful day," I heard Mother say. This was not exactly true- the grey in the sky was spreading like spilled paint- but Mother often believed things that were not exactly true and announced her belief in such a way that you wondered if it was you that was making the mistake.

"It's so hot," Marta said.

"You have water." Mother reminded.

Marta stuck her hands into the pockets of her shorts. "I can't drink it already," her voice was low and frustrated. I used to think there was nothing in the world Marta couldn't find a way to disagree with. This could leave me in turns irritated or infatuated with my older sister, depending on my mood.

We sloped up off the club course onto the road. Our city lay in front of us. Before we had even stepped off the plane, Mother was calling it "ours." It made me angry then, like she was trying to shrug our home off of us, a coat that no longer fit. I came to understand that this was the only way Mother could do it. Anything else would have torn her up inside in a way that would have spread to us instead of staying locked tightly at the back of her heart, the way it was then. I am not so naive now as to think she wasn't already torn up, just that she rarely let us guess it.

The air that day was cool and clean. To the left of the golf course lay the river. If you closed your eyes, you could hear the water crashing over itself trying to get to you. It made me think of the first thing I can remember- being at the ocean with Mother, Marta, the man who was my father. I remember a frayed orange blanket, a mouthful of salty water that stung my throat. I fought the urge to reach forward and grab Marta's hand.

We followed the road along the river. When I tried to veer off and walk alongside the yellow dotted lines of the road, Mother said in her singsong voice, "We are hiking only in a straight line, Aurelia."

We came to a house on the other side of the road. Marta and I passed this house nearly every day on our walk home from school. It had blue shutters and a dog that was sometimes tied to the lamppost with a loose rope. If I thought of it, I saved the crusts of my sandwiches for this dog. I realized that we were going to have to veer around the house, or else go into it, like the song they made the small children sing at the end of the school year- can't go over it, can't go under it, can't go around it, got to go through it!

I felt a dancing in my stomach. Mother had tied her brown hair back with a red bandanna. She was standing beside the lamppost where the dog sometimes was. Her arms were crossed, and she was smiling a little.

"What are we doing?" Marta asked.

"We are going inside."

"We can't just go inside." Marta stood beside Mother, and from the back they were nearly the same.

"We can't go back, and we must go straight-"

"We *can* go back. I can see the house from here."

Mother and Marta shared a lot of things. They were both allergic to penicillin. They could both eat an entire bag of almonds in one sitting and tie the stem of a cherry into a knot with their tongues. But nothing wove them more tightly together than their stubbornness. It was almost a game. You could feel it in the air sometimes, an unspoken agreement to argue being the only thing they could agree upon: what radio station we would listen to on our way to the city, which outfit Marta should wear to a friend's birthday party, if Mother should try and fix her teeth. Sometimes I liked to sit back and listen to them, the hills and dips in their voices as soothing to me as a crib mobile to a baby. Sometimes I knew if I didn't step in they would argue themselves into a circle, the middle of which I would be stuck in until one of them gave up.

I stepped forward, careful to make one foot go right in front of the other, the white curve top of my canvas shoes touching the base of my heel. Mother and Marta were quiet. I raised my hand and knocked on the door. I did not think about who would open the door, or what I would say when they did.

Through the frosted glass of the door came padding footsteps, the metal itching of a lock unhitching. When the door opened, I was staring up at the shining forehead of a bald man.

"Hello," I said, before he could say anything. "I am Aurelia. My mother and sister and I are hiking in a very straight line, and we have to come through your house."

"Well." The man was wearing a gold watch. It was shiny, but in a different way than his forehead. He had put himself in the space between the door and the inside and I was worried he would send us away.

"Sometimes I give my lunch to your dog," I told him.

"Hiking in a straight line, hm?" He made the space wider. I hesitated and then stepped inside. The white of my shoes against the blue carpet looked like a cloud.

"It was my mother's idea." Marta gave him.

"Interesting. I belonged to a hiking club at college."

"Were you allowed to walk in more than one direction?" Marta asked.

"Sometimes," he said, in the voice that adults use when they think children are younger than they really are. Rooms fell on either side of the blue carpet, one with a piano and a wall of books, another with an unmade bed. We stopped in the back room, which was the kitchen. There were photographs pinned to the fridge with magnets- a little boy with curly hair in his school uniform, an old woman I had never seen before, holding the dog. "Would you like some tea?" he asked.

Mother laughed. She used to say that here, there was no problem people could not solve by making a cup of tea. The first time I had tea was our first day here. Before we came to our house, we stayed in the city with a woman Mother went to school with back at home. The woman introduced herself to us as our *ciotka*. She had soft, doughy skin and bristly hair above her top lip that itched when she kissed my cheek. We sat at the table in her kitchen while she filled a red kettle with water from the sink. She took out four tea cups from her cupboard. They were white, with gold handles, and a pattern of roses that danced around the widest part of the cup. When the water boiled, our *ciotka* clamped a dish cloth over the handle of the kettle and steam poured out into the cups. She heaped sugar and milk into each one. In a language that sounded like the product of a car crash between Polish and English, she told us this was how 'they' drank it here. It occurred to me that 'they' was now 'us'. We stayed there a few months, but I remember little from that time in my life: Marta and I learned to take the bus down to the river, we ate bacon sandwiches on warm bread, we played with the other children who lived on the street.

"Yes, please," I said to the man. "Tea would be nice."

The man, he told us his name was Robert, took out a red cracker tin and from the tin he produced four tea bags. In the way that strangers sometimes seem comfortable sharing the fabric of their lives with you, Robert shook the cracker tin a little and said, "My wife bought this at a church sale. She never used things the way you're supposed to. For example, she put flowers in empty champagne bottles; for example, she made candleholders from pages of old books." Robert spoke like he was reading words off a page, but he moved around his kitchen like he was the only one in it.

"Did you lose your wife?" Mother asked.

"In a way." Robert took out the milk carton and dropped four small spoons into the tea cups. Dark water splashed over the rim of the cup where the spoons fell. "She got sick. She has to go away quite often." I prayed Mother wouldn't ask what was wrong with Robert's wife or where she went away to. He handed us each a cup.

Marta was silent. She skated away from strong emotion like a child avoiding the thin part of a frozen lake. Once, when we were small, I wandered away from our house to play by the water and I forgot to tell anybody. Marta found me a short while later. Her cheeks were flushed, wisps of hair flying around her face. She ran over to me and stepped, hard, on my bare foot. Years later, we would talk about this moment and she would tell me she was so terrified something bad had happened to me. When she saw I was alright she said she wanted to hold me to her but something inside her wouldn't allow it.

We drank our tea mostly in silence. "You have a lovely home," Mother said.

Robert smiled. The dog, whose name Robert told us was Pepper, trotted into the kitchen. "These fine ladies share their lunch with you," Robert told Pepper. Pepper rubbed up against Robert's leg.

"Usually it's just Aurelia that shares," Marta said, and I could have hugged her.

"The lady in the photograph-" I was nervous, and when I got nervous, my words ran into each other. "The lady in the photograph with Pepper," I pointed to the picture on the fridge. "Her. She is your wife?"

Robert set his cup down and walked over to the fridge. He lifted his index finger and, so gently I was not sure if he had even touched the picture, traced the outline of her face. It was a moment of such isolating intimacy that I felt I should turn away. "That is she. My Emily. She used to get so angry after, when she was first diagnosed. Her clothes grew too big for her. She hemmed the sleeves of her cardigans and she had to buy all new trousers, her waist got so small. Then one day I said to her- I said, 'Emily, why are you so upset? You are alive and thank God for that.' And she said, 'Robert, you're right.' And then-" he mimed snapping his fingers.

"Then, what?" Marta asked.

"Then she cheered up," he said simply.

The man who was my father got sick, too. He stopped going to work and started sleeping all day. He wore thick, grey socks and he was cold even when his skin was hot to the touch. Mother boiled the bedsheets in a pot on the stove, Marta and I had to play outside, quietly, and often we slept in the neighbours' houses, shuffled from bed to bed like rotating cards in a deck nobody wanted. I don't remember my father dying and I don't remember the funeral. After it was over, and we came home from the church, Mother went to bed for two days. She came downstairs on the morning of the second day. Marta and I were lying on our stomachs playing *mizerka.* Mother went into the kitchen and made pancakes. She sliced bananas and with the flat end of a knife, she broke up a bar of dark chocolate. When one side of the pancakes turned golden, she pressed the bananas and the chocolate down before flipping them over in the pan. She put the stack of pancakes in one of the empty glass trays, which yesterday or the day before yesterday or a hundred years ago had been a casserole or a lasagna in the hands of a *ciotka* dressed in black. "Well," Mother had said, in the same voice she would use four years later in Robert's kitchen. We ate the pancakes with our hands and fell asleep on the couch, legs overlapping each other, tangled yarn.

Mother turned on the tap and was washing the teacups. She set them upside down in the drying rack. "Well, girls." This was the way she put a ribbon on conversations. "Robert, thank you for the tea. I will say prayers for your Emily." Robert let us out his back door.

"The next time you want to give Pepper your lunch, you can knock on the door." Robert told me. "I hope the rest of your hike goes well."

Last week, I was at the supermarket, buying peaches for a pie I was making for my husband's birthday and I overheard a woman telling her friend that her son couldn't find a job because the "Poles had taken all of his." I opened my mouth to say something, wondering if slivers of my accent from childhood would pierce through my words, hoping they might. For my mother, whose hands I will always remember rolling out dough onto our flour covered kitchen counter, hands that were rough and red and smelled of ammonia- for the man who was my father, who slipped away from his life before I could ever know him- for Marta, who spent our first three months at school screaming at anybody who said I spoke strangely- I wanted to speak out. "I am Polish," I said to them, quietly. They did not hear me, or at least if they did they pretended they hadn't. My hands were buried in the bin of peaches and the two women were gone before I could say any more.

That day, we left Robert's backyard and walked through the street, now in reversed order: me, Marta, Mother. I wondered how we looked to anybody watching. I wondered what Robert and Pepper were going to have for lunch. It felt good to be in front.

My Father's House

That morning, her younger brother nudged open her door and got into bed beside her. It was something they used to do when they were small; she was terrified of thunderstorms and could use Derek's trembling hands, illuminated against her ladybug bed sheets by flashes of lightning, to convince herself she was doing him a favour by letting him sleep beside her. Derek was twelve now: he spent most of his time in the spare bedroom playing video games about stealing cars and killing other guys who stole cars. He said "fuck" when their mother wasn't around, but still slept with the blanket their Aunt Trish gave him when he was born. Other than last summer when they went to Washington and only had a single hotel room for the four of them, they had not shared a bed in probably five years. Then everything happened, and in the last few months she could usually count on him showing up. Sometimes she'd wake in the middle of the night to him breathing heavily beside her, and other times it was nearly daylight when he'd arrive. "Anna?" he said. His elbow was digging into her side. "What?" she didn't want to be annoyed with him, but she was. "Nothing. Just checking."

She remembered the morning they brought Derek home from the hospital. It was two days before her fifth birthday. Her mom said, "An early present!" Anna wanted a sister and spent the ride home glaring at the wrinkly boy who screamed in the car-seat beside her. "Take it back. I want a Barbie Dream House." They used to tell him that story and he'd cover his ears and pout.

"We should probably get up," he said.

"I know."

"I don't want to."

"I know."

Derek turned over, so his back was facing Anna. "I think Mom's going crazy."

"She's not crazy. She's depressed. We're all a little depressed."

"I'm not depressed. Only crazy people are depressed. I woke up last night because I could hear her singing on the porch. It was three o'clock in the morning."

"What was she singing?"

"Not the point."

It kind of was, but Anna let him have it. If she was singing "Thunder Road", it was probably about their Dad; if she was singing, like, "Mamma Mia", then maybe she had lost it a little. "Did you go out to her?" she asked.

He was quiet for a moment. "No. I wanted to, but I didn't know what to say."

Anna understood that. The winter she was fourteen her mother broke her wrist. She was taking casserole to their neighbour Lil because they'd just had a big storm and Lil didn't like to drive when the weather was bad. Liesel had been leaving Lil's and slipped on a patch of ice on the front porch steps. A week later, Anna was in the basement helping her mom with laundry. Liesel dropped a sock on the floor and she couldn't pick it up because of the cast. She started to cry. Anna picked up the sock, handed it sheepishly to her mother and went upstairs to get her dad. There was something unsettling about a moment that made your mother seem like anybody besides your mother.

"That's okay," she said.

His shoulder blades, bony and raised under the fabric of his Spiderman t-shirt, moved up and down. "She went back to sleep, I think. Not in her room." He added, though it wasn't necessary; their mother hadn't slept in her bedroom in a while. She created the illusion of it in the beginning, making a show of closing her door and turning the lights off. Once she thought Anna and Derek were asleep, she would go sleep on the couch and then was awake before either of them could accuse her of it. Eventually it got so Liesel couldn't even go into her room anymore, which struck Anna as kind of backwards, and she made up a bed for herself on the couch. "It's exciting!" she said. "Like camping!" Everything her mother said seemed to end with an exclamation now, like she was trying to make up for how she felt by injecting artificial joy into how she spoke.

"It'll be different soon," Anna promised. She didn't know if this was true, but she also didn't know what else to say.

"We really should get up," Derek said again. "I know," she said again. The movers were coming at noon. It was just after seven, but they still had to pack most of the stuff from their parents' room. They went to the grocery store yesterday and loaded the trunk up with empty boxes. When they came home, Liesel frowned a little, touched Anna's hair and said, "You didn't have to do that! I could have gone." Anna nodded. "I know, Mom, but we were out already."

Derek sighed and sat up. "Okay."

Anna reached over and ran her fingers up and down his back, the way she used to when he was little. "Okay," she echoed.

***

From her place on the picnic table, she could see her mother in the kitchen. She was dicing cucumbers on a cutting board, a cloth resting in the crook of her neck, boxes piled on the counter behind her. When Anna looked at Liesel, she saw the same woman she'd seen her entire life: curly hair and a smile that shone through her eyes because she was embarrassed about the crookedness of her teeth. Anna saw an unchanging, effervescent woman, she smelled St. Ives hand cream and vanilla. It was only when she looked at photographs- her mother draped over a wicker chair, wearing leg warmers and one of Anna's dad's t-shirts, her mother and Anna's grandfather sitting on the stoop of her mother's childhood home- that she realized her mother had aged. She noticed the subtle fading of the colour of her hair, the deepening of lines around her eyes.

The wood of the table had sagged and darkened with the seasons; her dad built it the summer they moved in. Eighteen years of meals, snowfalls, wide eyes peeking out from underneath in furtive games of hide and seek. The large green umbrella stood in its centre, faded with the heat of the sun, a wind-chime and a clumsily constructed plant-holder hanging tentatively from opposing corners. Back in March, when they decided to leave, Anna childishly asked Liesel if they couldn't maybe take the table with them.

Liesel looked up at Anna and smiled. She swept the cucumbers onto a folded paper towel, crossed the kitchen and slid open the screen door. "Isn't it exciting?" Liesel asked brightly, sitting down beside her daughter.

"What?"

"All of it. Getting to go someplace different and start everything again."

The hair on Anna's arms prickled, but she smiled and said, "Yeah. It is." Derek was in the backyard kicking around a soccer ball he'd found underneath the deck. Her heart ached with the knowledge that he would get older and she would be unable to protect him from everything, from anything. "It might be hard," Anna offered. She regretted the words as soon as she'd said them. She could almost see them being nailed into the wall Liesel was busy building around herself.

Liesel squeezed Anna's kneecap gently. "You wanna check your room again? Make sure you've got everything?"

Anna wanted to stay sitting with her mother, to find the words that would make everything right again. Instead, she nodded and went inside. She knew she had everything packed. She had made lists for her and Derek, they labelled boxes and wrapped coffee mugs in newspapers. Derek put his X-Box in a battered green suitcase and secured it a spot in the backseat of the car. He said he didn't trust the movers. "They won't steal it," Anna assured him. "You can't know that," Derek said gravely. Anna knew everything was packed and knew that she hadn't forgotten anything, but she went up to her room anyway.

Her parents moved into their house when Anna was three months old. Her bedroom had been her bedroom since then. Her father built her crib and her mother painted the walls. After the crib, the first thing in Anna's room was a framed photograph of Bruce Springsteen, cut out from a Rolling Stone article. It was a small picture, in a thick yellow frame. The frame was adorned with clay roses and a teddy bear. The teddy bear was on the bottom left corner of the frame and stuck out, his head tilted to the right, so that it looked like he was watching Bruce Springsteen perform. Anna's dad used to say that the man in the photo was her Uncle Bruce and until she was thirteen this was what she told people whenever they asked about it.

For most of the summers that Anna could remember, Liesel would leave for work just as James was coming home. He worked in the Toyota car plant a half hour from their house: two weeks of midnight shifts, then two weeks of day shifts, overtime on most Saturdays. He always had a book in his lunch bag, something about the Civil War or Nelson Mandela's autobiography or the history of the fast food industry. Liesel worked part time at the YMCA from June to September so that she could be home with Anna and Derek during the day. From September to June she worked cleaning houses.

In Grade Three, they had Career Day. Anna proudly dedicated half a Bristol board to photos of her father and car parts and the other half to photos of her mother and mop buckets. When she stood up in front of her class, a girl in the front row pointed at the pictures of her mom and proclaimed, "Hey! That lady cleans my house." Anna could not have said, truthfully, if she'd been embarrassed by this. She spent so much of her time trying to pretend like it didn't bother her that her dad was the smartest man she knew but that he worked sixty hours a week putting together parts for a car that they didn't have the money for. She didn't want to think about her mom scrubbing dirt out of someone else's bathroom floor.

James would come home, his fingernails dirty, smelling of coffee and hot metal. They'd eat burgers or hotdogs or pasta that Liesel had made for them. Sometimes on Fridays they ordered pizza. After dinner, Anna and Derek would walk a block and a half to the public pool and swim until Liesel was finished work. She picked them up on her way home and then let them watch a half hour of cartoons before bed.

One Saturday in the beginning of August, James woke Anna and Derek up. It was still dark outside. "Get up. We're going to the beach today," he told them. It was supposed to have been his eighth consecutive Saturday of overtime. When Liesel came home from work the night before, they lay on top of their bed, the ceiling fan working furiously above them. "I think I'm gonna call in sick tomorrow," he said. Liesel snaked her leg underneath his. "You get time and a half," she reminded him. "I know. The kids have been in that pool every night for two months. I want to go to the lake."

They had lunch at a diner on the strip and Anna and Derek were allowed to order ice cream after. James filled a plastic bucket with water and ran it over Anna's feet when they got too warm from the sand. They played Marco Polo and Colours and Spud. The backs of Derek's legs got sunburnt and he slept lying face down in the car. Anna, Liesel and James sang the whole way home. Her parents had their windows rolled down and Liesel kept looking over her shoulder into the backseat, making sure it wasn't too windy. Anna fell asleep at some point, her bathing suit damp and itchy underneath her shorts. She woke up in bed, wearing clean pyjamas. Her skin stung a little, but her eyes weren't sore the way they were after the pool.

Later, Derek would say that this had been a Good Day. He said it definitively, like there could only be days that were good and then days that were bad. The day they saw the big T-Rex at the Smithsonian was a Good Day, the day Dad got laid off was a Bad Day. The Friday before they were to move, Derek was lying upside down on her bed. "I think that when Dad left, he took all the Good Days... fucking asshole." They laughed until their stomachs hurt, because it was better than crying.

***

He left two days after Derek's final hockey game. Derek had been playing rotary hockey every winter since he was six. Their games were Saturday mornings at seven thirty. Liesel went to every single one. Anna went a few times a year and sat in the heated area outside the arena. She knew Derek was number seven and that it cost two dollars for a Styrofoam cup of hot chocolate from the stand downstairs. Liesel wore James' winter jacket and gloves and paced up and down inside the arena. She knew the names of all the kids on Derek's team. "Go Michael, c'mon Kennedy, PASS Jordan, PASS." Whenever Derek scored, which usually happened two or three times a season, Liesel would jump up and down and scream. The other parents looked at her like she was one of those mothers that projected her unfulfilled desire to be an NHL star onto her eight-year-old, but Liesel wouldn't have cared if Derek was playing hockey or dodgeball or mini-golf. If it made him happy, she would pace and jump and scream for him.

James went to all the games when he wasn't working and tried to make up for the ones he missed by making plans with Derek about plays he might try for next week. James would yell numbers where Liesel would yell names, and would cry, "That was offside!" or "You're giving him a penalty for THAT?" at the referees, who were usually boys Anna went to school with. No matter how well or how poorly Derek played, James would wait outside the dressing room after the game, bump him on the shoulder and say, "Buddy, you were a star."

Derek's team this year had been particularly good. They were playing to win first place. It was the first game in a while that all of them would be at together. At breakfast, James asked if he was nervous. Derek shrugged. "I don't care," he said. Anna heard Derek in his bedroom the night before, watching Sidney Crosby videos and slapping a plastic puck against the back of his door with his stick. He slept with his pyjamas on inside out because he had heard it was good luck.

Anna sat inside the arena this time, a few rows in front of where her parents were standing. "I really hope they win," Liesel confessed to James. James had been laid off from the factory six weeks ago. He was eligible for unemployment but not severance pay. "Me too," he said. The night of the lay-off he got drunk and sat on the couch and cried. The next morning, he said he had a good feeling it would only be two weeks, tops. The night after that, he got drunk again. He cried some more and told Anna he was sorry. Her mom made Anna and Derek go over to Lil's. Liesel was trying to see if she could pick up a few extra shifts at the YMCA. James told her it wasn't necessary, that he'd be back at the factory before the kids finished school for the summer. Anna came downstairs after dinner one night to her dad sitting at the kitchen table with the newspaper. He was circling Help Wanted ads: a pizza company looking for a delivery person, a restaurant that wanted a dishwasher. "Just temporary," he said with a smile. "Until something better comes along."

Both teams were warming up now, showing off for each other. The shoulder pads and bulky helmets and the height of the blades on their skates made them seem older than they were. They were all pounding each other on the back and slapping their sticks together. Every so often, one of them would start chanting their team name and then the other players would join in. Because they were rotary kids, their teams were sponsored by local businesses. This year they were the Drill-Technologies, last year they had been the Little Beaver Web Designs. Names like the Warriors and the Hawks were reserved for teams in the competitive league.

One of the referees blew their whistle and dropped the puck onto the ice. Derek was on defense today. His team scored twice within the first ten minutes. The first time, Liesel cheered so loudly that one of the dads asked if the boy was her son. By the end of the first period, they had scored twice more. "This is really it," James said. "If the blue team-"

"Steel Automotive," Liesel interjected.

"If the blue team decides that they've lost, then it's done."

"They've only been playing for like, twenty minutes. They could come back." Anna said. She didn't know why she was making things difficult.

"They could, yeah, but what I'm saying is that if they give up now then Derek's won."

Derek's team did win. The final score was 6-1: the one goal they gave up was sort of a result of Derek's poor defense skills, but there seemed to be an agreement amongst the three of them not to mention it. They went to a room upstairs after so the coaches could hand out the medals, little steel circles attached to flimsy bits of red and white fabric. There was nothing distinguishing these medals from the participation ones that the last place team would receive, but Derek wore it around his neck all day.

Later, Anna would retrace every part of this day, trying to decide if there was a moment when her father knew for certain he was leaving. She thought about it so often that she was sure she had altered the way things actually happened, positive that she was missing something. She'd read once that every time you recalled a memory your brain changed it a little, so that eventually none of the things you remembered happened the way you thought they had. Her earliest memory, or at least what she perceived to be her earliest memory, was of being three, maybe four years old, and sitting underneath the Christmas tree in the front hall. Dad was crouched on the tiled floor in front of her. He had borrowed a tape recorder from their next door neighbour and was filming her singing carols that they'd learned at school last week.

"Rudolph the red-nosed RAIN dear-"

"Reindeer-"

"That's what I said, Daddy."

Anna didn't know if she actually remembered this conversation, or if she had just watched the tape enough to think she did, but the next part she knew she would have remembered, with or without the video: the sound of boots kicking against the outside door, a burst of cold air, the rusted jingle bells clanging against one another. Mom stepped inside, her cheeks looked warm but would feel cold and her hair was covered in tiny white flakes of snow that seemed to melt every time Anna got a look at them. Dad got up from the floor and swung the tape recorder towards Mom. She set grocery bags down on the floor, "Careful James, there's bread in that one," she warned as Dad crossed the hall to kiss her.

Anna always felt that she had to be all that her parents were not. Her mother was painfully shy in high school, so Anna joined the debate team even though public speaking made her want to throw up. Liesel would say, with a kind of pride that lingered on the threshold of intimidation, "I can't imagine doing that when I was your age." James never went to college, so by the time Anna was in the tenth grade she was going to university fairs and collecting brochures from schools she thought she would like. Her dad could go to the corner store for milk and spend twenty minutes talking to whoever was working, but this was one thing he did not know how to discuss. He would always say tentatively, "So, a guy at work was telling me that his niece is in that one program you mentioned", like he was never sure if he was making sense or not. Anna's parents never demanded that she be any of these things, but she believed that if she wasn't they would feel that they'd failed her somehow.

The memory, the tree and Dad and Mom and the songs, was perfectly ordinary. There was no reason it should have stayed with her the way it had and yet when she saw that the picture was gone, and knew that he was gone, it was the first thing she thought of. She kept remembering, with a vividness that almost confused her, the way her Dad had been listening to her sing and the way the pine needles bent gently into the curve of her spine as she sat, cross-legged, back pressed into the tree. Everything felt right.

***

Derek finished in the backyard with the soccer ball and was upstairs with Anna. They were sitting in her room. "Mom's saying bye to Lil," Derek told her. "Kind of dumb. We're only moving across town."

"She's old. It might be a while before they see each other again."

"Mom isn't that old." Derek was laughing before he'd even finished his joke and then was straight faced again just as quickly. "If it matters, they'll see each other."

"Is that about Dad?"

"No. It's about Mom and Lil."

"Just because Dad left doesn't mean you don't matter."

"I know that."

"And it wasn't your fault."

"I know that, too."

They were quiet again for a while. It was the last time they would be in her bedroom as her bedroom. A couple who was expecting their first child bought their house. "It's got such great potential," the dad said. "I think we can do a lot with it." The mom said they were going to paint Anna's bedroom and turn it into an office. Derek's bedroom would be the nursery.

"Do you think we'll see him again?" he asked. Derek had been at his friend's house the day it happened. Anna finished school at three and it took her fifteen minutes to walk home. The first thing she'd noticed was that the car was gone. Liesel was usually done cleaning by the time school got out and it had been a while since James had taken the car anywhere.

Anna held her breath. "I don't know." The second thing she'd noticed was how cold the house was. She thought maybe her parents had gone to get groceries and had turned the heating off when they left. "Do you hope we will?" she asked him.

She'd put down her backpack and called out, "Mom?" Anna went into the kitchen. There was broken glass on the floor. Her dad's coat, which usually hung on the back of the chair at the breakfast bar, wasn't there. "Dad?" The TV had been left on in the living room.

"Is it bad if I do?" Derek's voice was shaking.

When she'd gone upstairs, she found Liesel sitting on the floor outside of her and James' bedroom. "Mom? What's going on?" Liesel looked up. "Your father's gone." Anna crouched down beside her. "Are you okay? What do you mean Dad's gone?" "I mean he's gone. Jesus, Anna. He left."

"No, buddy. You can be mad but still want to see him again."

Anna had stood in the hall in front of her mom and called their Aunt Trish, but it went straight to voicemail. "Mom? What do you want me to do?" Anna turned seventeen last month but, in that moment, she felt like a child. "Mom?" "Go away, Anna. Please, sweetheart. Just for a minute." Anna went into her bedroom. The yellow clay frame, the photo of Bruce Springsteen, was gone. It had stood on the cream coloured desk in front of her window for her entire life. In its place was an envelope with her name on it. It was her dad's handwriting. Anna took the envelope and put it in the bottom of her backpack.

Derek nodded. "Do you want to see him too?"

Anna didn't know what she wanted. She didn't know what Derek wanted or needed to hear. She wished she didn't have to think about these kinds of things. "Yeah. I think so." She didn't know if her dad left a letter for Derek or for her mom. She didn't know where he was living. She asked Liesel about it once. Liesel clapped her hands squarely on Anna's shoulders. "I don't know, baby. Let's not talk about it," she said.

"I heard Aunt Trish telling Mom she thinks he had a breakdown," Derek offered up. The unspoken hope here was that if this were true, then he hadn't exactly left because he wanted to.

"Maybe he did."

"Maybe not."

The movers came right at noon. Derek put a case of bottled water on the front porch for them. Liesel hovered around them nervously for a little while and then joined Derek and Anna on the porch. They were standing off to the side, watching the men walk into and out of their house, loading boxes and mattresses and chairs into the back of the white truck.

"This is weird," Derek said.

Liesel linked her arm through his. "I know."

Anna thought of her first debate competition, when the tips of her fingers were wet with perspiration and she felt like she might pass out. Liesel brought her flowers and told her how well she'd done. All she'd wanted to do was tell her mom that it had been the worst two hours of her life, and then Liesel said, "I never would have been brave enough for that."

"I wish Dad was here," she said finally.

There was a silence. Liesel linked her other arm through Anna's. "I know."

Learning to Fall

In Grade Five health, we learned about the miracle of life. Our teacher showed us a cartoon diagram of a fetus in utero- the rest of the woman's body was the colour of wet sand, but her stomach was dark red. A little baby was curled up inside it.

"Any questions, class?" she asked us.

"Does having a baby hurt?"

"It does."

"How much?"

Before she could answer, another kid jumped in. "Does it hurt more or less than breaking your arm?"

"Or is it like getting your leg cut off?"

When we are small, we think painful experiences can have a grade attached to them- being stabbed in the throat is worse than being punched in the face is worse than falling off your bike is worse than stubbing your toe.

When I was a kid, the most painful thing that ever happened to me was also the best thing that ever happened to me. I was seven years old the summer the circus came to town. June and I begged for three days straight for our dad to take us. He said no for two and a half days straight. "It's animal cruelty," he told us.

My dad was very big on animal cruelty that summer; he'd watched a documentary about whales in captivity and anytime June or I talked about going to Marineland, my dad would ask us how we'd like it if we had to live in a tiny cage all day while whales watched us. Once, June had shrugged and said, "That sounds kind of cool." We went to the grocery store one night. June and I made a beeline for the meat department, the way we usually did. Beside the glass cases of smoked ham and turkey breast and summer sausage was a fish tank. They kept lobsters inside the tank. Each lobster had a little white tag tied around their claws. Sometimes, if they floated around the top of the tank, you could stand on your tip-toes and reach your hand in and try to touch their antennae. June and I lived in constant hope that one day we would come into the grocery store and leave with a lobster. That particular night, our dad came over to get us once he was done shopping. He stared at the animals and shook his head. "Lobsters mate for life," he told us.

We saw a flyer advertising the circus on our way home from camp. We went to day camp at the church, not because my parents were religious, but because the church was down the block and my mom could stand on the front porch with Baby Tommy and watch us until we got in safely through the front doors.

The flyer was taped to a lamppost. It was covered in red and white stripes, with a photograph of a man wearing a tall black hat. A monkey sat on his shoulder. YOU WON'T BELIEVE YOUR EYES. We began our circus campaign the moment we got in the door. My dad barbecued corn for dinner that night, which was our least favourite thing to eat in the summer. It was too hot to hold, and the kernels got stuck in your teeth, and sometimes if Dad didn't shuck the husks properly, little bits of string slipped down your throat like hair. We promised our parents we would have corn on the cob every night for the rest of our lives if we were allowed to go to the circus.

Eventually, my mom told my dad that if he didn't take us to the circus and shut us up, she was moving out. So, after supper on

Friday, my dad and June and I walked up to the arena. Friday nights in the winter, we came to see hockey games here. My dad would buy us a slice of pizza at intermission, which was the main reason we came. After we'd eaten the pizza, and the Zamboni had made the ice look shiny again, June and I would go play in the heated area up above the arena. Sometimes, we lay by the radiator and were lulled into a warm sleep by the muted sound of skates stopping on ice, clapping, whistles blowing. When the game was over, and we were trying to find our car in the crowded parking lot, the air biting our cheeks, Dad would hold June and I in each of his arms and carry us above his shoulders like trophies.

The circus came to town in the middle of July and I couldn't remember what it felt like to be cold. My parents said it was the hottest summer they could remember. Most nights, the five of us slept on a blow-up mattress in the living room in front of a fan. It was too hot upstairs, and the sound of the fan could sometimes put Baby Tommy to sleep. June and I waited until our parents had fallen asleep, and then we put the TV on. We fell asleep in front of the green glow of late-night cartoons.

The entire road around the arena was closed off and the parking lot was filled with trailers whose doors were swung open, piles of straw and worn blankets peeking out. Behind a barricade, a woman wearing blue jeans and a grey t-shirt was leading an elephant down to drink from the river. It was the most amazing thing I had ever seen. June and I stopped in unison and watched as it lowered its trunk down into the water. The elephant's left foot hovered cautiously on the riverbank and we watched as it lifted its trunk to put the water in its mouth.

We went inside, and Dad bought us a yellow tub of popcorn to share. We went to find our seats. The man from the flyer was walking around where the skating rink used to be. Instead of ice, he was walking on a yellow star. He was talking to the crowd and his voice seemed to be coming from every corner. "Ladies and gentlemen," he cried out. His voice put goosebumps on my arms. "Boys and girls." He waved at June and I when we sat down.

The lights dimmed after a while and in the moments of darkness, I waved my hands above my head and let out a little scream. When the lights came back on, a girl with blonde hair that fell to her hips stood on a horse and the horse ran in neat little circles around the arena and the girl with blonde hair stood upside down, one hand on the horse's white back. Seven men wearing matching red suits balanced like dominos on a bicycle and traded sticks of fire like secrets and a clown folded himself into a glass box and the elephant we'd seen drinking from the river stood on a barrel and rolled from the top of the yellow star down to the bottom.

The grand finale was an act called the cannonball man. A man wearing purple pants and a striped t-shirt exploded from a cannon and landed halfway across the arena, on a blue mat that was not unlike the ones that we practiced tumbling on in gym class. I guess there was probably a harness and a smoke machine and an Oz the Great and Powerful behind a screen, hitting a button that made a cannon sound at the exact right moment. But then, and still in my memory, the cannon brought that man into existence on its own.

On the way home, June and I told our dad all our favourite parts. We got the feeling he had seen a different kind of show than us. He looked away when the lion jumped through the flaming hoop, but when he tucked us into bed that night, he kissed each of our foreheads and said, "I'm really glad you girls had fun."

My sister and I talked about the circus all the next day. We cut a shoddy star from the cardboard box that our new refrigerator had been delivered in and we made our stuffed animals perform a great number of tricks for our dolls. We ate grilled cheese sandwiches under the trampoline and decided we would start our own circus. We figured that we should get started after dinner, and that we might as well begin with a bang.

We stood on the back deck, which was raised probably fifteen feet above our backyard. Our mom was in bed with Baby

Tommy and Dad had gone to get the newspaper. We decided we would jump off the deck to get a feel for what it was like to be the cannonball man.

"It's the grand finale," June rationalized. "If we do this first, all the other stuff will seem easy."

I don't remember the first time I felt fear, but I'm certain it wasn't then, standing on the back deck with my sister. June went first. She landed with a gentle thud, her legs bent, her bare feet little tan bumps in the grass. I went next, with slightly less grace. I landed almost exactly on my face. My nose took the brunt of my fall. I don't remember much- June screaming, blood falling into the back of my throat, the nurse giving me a banana popsicle.

On the way home from the hospital, tucked into my dad's coat, Tommy in his car seat beside us, my mom asked, "What were you thinking?"

"I was flying." I told her.

I think June was sort of annoyed that I had broken my nose instead of her. Even though it was past midnight when we got home, my dad made me French toast. The doctor said I wasn't supposed to sleep for too long in case I had a concussion, so my dad and I slept alone on the couch and we watched cartoons. My dad woke me up every hour to make sure I still knew who I was. June had to sleep in our bedroom alone, which I knew she hated. A little part of me wanted to ask Dad if she couldn't come downstairs and sit with us, but a bigger part of me felt special and wanted to stay there, alone with my dad. The next morning the skin under my eyes looked bruised, and I caught June pressing her thumbs into her eyes, trying to bruise hers too. I pretended like I hadn't seen it.

I've never been to another circus since that summer, and I sort of hope I never will. There are some things that are magical and beautiful and perfect when you are small and if you revisit them only in memory, they can stay that way forever.

Unfinished

They didn't call it a memorial service, but that's what it was. The poster said it was a celebration of his life, the event invitation asked that everyone wear bright clothing because it's what he would have wanted. His mother wore red lipstick and a dress the colour of sunshine but the skin under her eyes was puffed and worn like an overripe peach and her hand was a shaking fist clenching a damp Kleenex.

The only other funeral Laurel had ever been to was in Grade Six, for the father of Nelson, a boy in her class. His dad had been vaguely sick for a while, bald head and sunken cheekbones, had sat courtside at their basketball tournament in a wheelchair with a blue quilt draped across his knees. One day, before lunch, Nelson started crying at his desk and their teacher let everyone go out to recess early. Later, during math class, Laurel silently slid his workbook from his desk to hers and answered the twelve problems they had been assigned for homework- it was the only way she could think to help. That summer, a girl in her class phoned all the other kids from the sixth grade and told them that Nelson's dad had died. The funeral was on a Sunday morning in mid-July. Laurel wore a black velvet dress that was too tight around the waist and the shoes from her first communion, now a size small. She stood with the other girls from her class and cried through all of Amazing Grace with the kind of sadness that comes when you realize for the first time that the people you love will eventually have to leave you- a selfish sadness to carry in your heart while you watch six young men carry the casket of a thirty-eight-year-old father out of a church. Nelson held his mother's hand all the way down the aisle after the service. His little sister, seven years old, blonde hair pinned back with a butterfly beret, had a run in her tights and waved at everyone in the pews. Laurel walked home after, ate a grilled cheese sandwich and played Gameboy with her younger brother, Curtis.

She was seventeen now. In ten days, she would begin her first year of university. Her bedroom was a cardboard imitation of a ransacked city. Boxes were bursting with socks and bottles of shampoo and clothes hangers, Ziploc bags hugging stacks of photographs and postcards and birthday cards, a bright green suitcase the metropolis centre of it all, empty except for a small pile of sweaters.

Last Tuesday, sitting cross-legged on her trampoline, she had checked her vibrating cellphone and read a text from Catherine- "Bailey's dead. Call me." She actually laughed- of course Bailey wasn't dead.

The night before last, Laurel ran into him while she was walking home from work. Copper hair, freckles slapped across his face like a cluster of stars. "Hey, loser," he was on his bike, but got off to walk beside her. They went to their high school, sat against the tree trunk at the top of the hill and smoked a joint. He tapped the joint with his index finger, ash sprinkling the grass, and laughed not unkindly when she gestured to the old yellow building behind them and said, "Don't you think it still feels like ours?"

"You're so sentimental," he rolled his eyes at her, but she took notice of the way his fingers trailed over the trunk when they stood up. Laurel held onto everything and Bailey let things go as soon as they were finished. Laurel ran down the hill with her arms thrown out. Bailey walked his bike on the gravel pavement beside her. He went home to have dinner with his girlfriend and she went home to get drunk with Catherine.

The sky was the colour of cotton candy, a sheath of pink and swirls of blue. The sun was setting, bursts of colour seeping through the spaces between the trees that dotted the edge of town. Winters when Laurel and Curtis were younger, they used to come here after school and toboggan. Their dad would stand on the back deck and whistle when it was time to come home for dinner.

Two days later, Laurel had read the text from Catherine once and felt nothing. She went inside, poured herself a glass of orange juice, drank it, put the empty glass in the sink and walked downtown to the store where Addie worked in the summer. They sold things like knee high socks with the word BALLSACK printed on them in block letters and old rotary dial telephones and handmade Christmas cards that cost eleven dollars. Addie was sitting on a wooden stool behind the counter, her black hair in a thick braid that rested on her shoulder. Laurel felt a pulse of energy in her stomach.

"Catherine said that Bailey died." Laurel was chewing a stick of gum and she had to fight the urge to blow a bubble.

"What?"

"Bailey. Catherine said he died."

Addie was crying instantly, and Laurel craved this kind of emotion. "What happened?" Addie snagged a loose thread from her t-shirt in the cash register as she hurried to lock it, quivering fingers knocking over a plastic stand of scented pencils.

"A drug. A kind of drug. It was laced." Laurel hated saying this. How many times had they read about some kid who had experimented with a new drug and been killed by it, rolled their eyes at the stupidity as a school photo and a name flashed by on the ticker tape of the six o'clock news, talking about something else before it could even cut to commercials.

Addie locked up the store. Her mom came to pick her up and Laurel went home. She went to the movies with Curtis and when she came home she said to her mother, Maggie, "You know Bailey?"

"The little redhead?"

She nodded. "He's dead. Catherine told me this afternoon."

"Oh, baby." Her mother hovered uncertainly for a moment and came to Laurel. Maggie hugged her fiercely and for some reason Laurel thought of the first time she'd gotten her period. She was eleven, the first girl in her class to start. She had worn pink corduroy pants to school and bled a red, wet circle right through the crotch of them. She didn't know what was happening to her until her teacher handed her a pair of blue gym shorts and a box of tampons. When she came home from school and told her mom what happened, her cheeks hot and the inside of her thighs crusted with dried blood, her mother hugged her in the same way she was hugging her now. Laurel could cry for half an hour over a dead bird she'd seen on the side of the street, but she found it intensely difficult to be vulnerable with the things that really mattered.

"Do you want to talk about it?" Maggie asked.

Laurel shook her head, shrugged out of her mother's embrace. "I kinda just want to sleep. Maybe in the morning. Night Mama," she kissed Maggie's cheek, soft and warm, and went upstairs.

Laurel got into bed but did not sleep. Later, she heard something hitting her window pane: Catherine and Addie were sitting on the curb outside her house. It had been the three of them for a long time. Catherine lived two doors down from Laurel. The two of them spent childhood summers camping in Laurel's backyard, lips stained dark from picking blueberries out of their neighbour's garden, lying in the bed of Catherine's dad's pick-up truck eating popsicles that dripped down their wrists and matted the hair on their arms. Addie came a little later, quiet and sweet, falling into their lives so seamlessly that after a short time they couldn't remember themselves without her. Friday nights the

74

three of them watched movies in Addie's living room. Her mom made them popcorn in a pot on the stove and when Addie's parents weren't watching, they took turns pressing their fingers to the side of the plastic bowl, gathering up flecks of salt and warm, wet butter, dribbling the mixture into their mouths.

Laurel put on shoes, closed her front door quietly behind her. She sat down wordlessly in between them. Catherine cupped a metal thermos in her hands, fingers woven together around it. She offered it to Laurel. Laurel took a sip and coughed. It tasted peppery but spread a warmth to her chest when she swallowed.

"Whiskey from my dad," Catherine said.

"He gave it to you?"

"Hell no," she laughed.

"I don't know what to do." Addie's voice was small. "It doesn't feel right to just sit here."

"We sat Shiva for my grandma when she died." Catherine offered, running a finger along the rim of the thermos.

"Bailey's not even Jewish."

"I'm just saying. It sucked anyway. I couldn't shower for like, a week."

Laurel picked up a pebble that was wedged underneath her shoe. She held it in between her thumb and index finger, shutting one eye until everything but the pebble was blurry. "I don't feel anything," she said quietly. "I don't feel like it's possible for him to be dead. I just keep expecting him to show up and laugh about what a good joke this all was."

"Denial," Catherine nodded.

Laurel had to stop herself from rolling her eyes. "Maybe."

"My mom said the funeral is Friday," Addie said. "Just his family. Forrest. There's a memorial service after that." In the same way that Laurel had Catherine and Addie, Bailey had Forrest. Forrest's uncle lived out west. He'd offered the two of them jobs working at a ski lodge for that coming winter- they were supposed to leave the day after Laurel started university.

Laurel dropped the pebble and scooped up a pile of small, gritty rocks, instead. She cupped her hands around them and slowly drew her fingers apart so that the rocks began to fall through the pockets of air, hitting the sidewalk gently at first and then harder as she drew them further and further apart.

***

"I really think you should go back and change." Maggie said nervously. Laurel privately agreed but also believed if she took the dress off she would be incapable of putting anything else back on.

"It'll be fine, Mom." She was wearing a cream coloured dress, patterned with big flowers. Reaching up to fix her hair in the car, she'd torn the fabric underneath her left armpit.

"You're sure you don't want me to come in?"

Laurel did, in a desperate sense, want her mother to come in with her and yet was glad she wasn't. Maggie had frozen large Tupperware containers of spaghetti and dropped them off at Bailey's house that morning. His funeral had been late last week. He'd been cremated. Laurel didn't know what they'd done with his ashes, didn't really want to know just yet, but was glad at least that she didn't have to picture his body underground, suffocating soil and a gravestone with a tiny dash in between the date of his birth and death which was meant to represent the entirety of Bailey's life.

The funeral home was a long white building on the edge of town, tucked in between a real estate office and a convenience store. The back was floor to ceiling windows, overlooking an open patch of grass and a church. They used to come out here to play hide and seek and once Laurel had hidden at the back of the funeral home, crouched down in the grass. She had been overcome with fear at the realization that she was looking into a building which housed corpses and had lain with her eyes tightly closed until she'd been found.

Maggie pulled into the circular driveway and touched her daughter's cheek gently. "Call me if you want a ride home."

Laurel shut the car door, conscious of the breeze tickling her underarm through the hole in the dress. The heels of her shoes clicked against the linoleum floor and she wished she could just take them off. Inside the hall there was a large, framed photo of Bailey. Ski goggles hung from his neck, the hazy outline of a snowy hill looming behind him. He wasn't staring right at the camera but was smiling anyway. Voices grew louder, heading towards her, and she hurried past the photograph and the group of people to whom the voices belonged.

Inside, mounted televisions played a series of videos Bailey and Forrest had been making since Bailey's grandfather bought him a camcorder for his fourteenth birthday. Laurel remembered Bailey lugging the camera with him, filming them lying in the grass by the river, making drinks in Catherine's kitchen, walking home from school.

On the television, a young Forrest was tumbling over a frozen river, clutching at his hockey stick. You could hear him laughing underneath the sound of Bailey's prepubescent voice narrating squeakily- "This is Forrest in the midst of believing he's got any talent as a hockey player." His voice was muffled from the wind, his red gloved hand reaching in front of the camera to brush snow from the lens. "Here we have the wild Bailey in his natural habitat," Forrest with a terrible Australian accent at the bottom of a ski hill, a moving dot on the hill slowly turning into Bailey,

"Crikey! Would you look at that!" A wooden frame filled with family photos hung in the middle of two of the televisions- old pictures of Bailey and his sister on their deck wearing yellow sweaters and holding handmade paper turkeys, Bailey laughing atop his dad's shoulders, Bailey as a toddler sitting on a leather couch holding a half-eaten pear in his lap.

Laurel scanned the room, desperate for someone she knew. Hands waved at her and she moved automatically toward them. The hands belonged to a group of girls from her school. They stood in a semi-circle and reminded Laurel of penguins in a blizzard. Teary eyed, they hugged Laurel in turns. "Such a tragedy," one of them lamented. "I just wish I'd gotten to know him better." She said, smudging a dollop of lip gloss. Laurel felt like she might be sick. "It totally makes you think, y'know? I'm so lucky it wasn't any of you guys." Laurel could not, with any confidence, have said what this girl's name was. Quietly, she excused herself and went out the side door.

Outside, patches of grass were brightened by pools of sunlight and the flowers in the small garden were cheerful. It was one of those late August days which would seem like a dream come October. Bailey's sister was there, her arm looped tightly through her boyfriend's. She nodded at Laurel, her tight curls brushing against her shoulder.

Laurel found Forrest and went to him. They hugged. It felt foreign to hug Forrest- she had known him since Grade Nine, he taught her how to play beer pong and she helped him bake the cake for his mother's fiftieth birthday party. They knew each other intimately but not at all in this way. Forrest smiled at her when they pulled apart. Partly because she couldn't think of anything else to say and partly because she felt they needed it, she raised her arm, exposing the hole in her dress. "Am I not the worst?" He laughed, and she relaxed.

Crowds of people spilled outside every so often- the biology teacher from their high school hugged Bailey's sister, shook

Forrest's hand, Bailey's dad led his wife over to their daughter, the three of them stood together without speaking. Catherine and Addie appeared together and came to Laurel and Forrest.

"I should probably go in," Forrest said after some time had passed. "There's just so many people," his voice was shaky, and Addie reached out gently to hold his hand. Later, the four of them sat inside, a plate of untouched food in the middle of them. The general store where they went almost every day for lunch had provided sushi. A group of children were playing a strangely hushed version of tag, the videos of Bailey and Forrest now looped in silence. A white tablecloth was draped over a banquet table on top of which people were placing flowers and sympathy cards.

Quiet hung in the air as thick as heat and all Laurel could think about was the Christmas party Bailey threw for them that year. His dad carved an ice rink in the backyard and they'd helped his mother drape fairy lights from the snow topped trees. They toasted marshmallows around a tall bonfire. Their cold fingers clumsily broke off squares of chocolate and graham crackers and poured rum into coffee mugs full of warm apple cider. It hadn't been particularly different than any of their other parties. They'd wound up dancing in the living room, dancing badly, didn't care how they looked or how they sounded. Laurel had never been in love but felt that this was love in its purest definition- pushing aside couches and footstools, kicking off shoes and singing along to the songs they'd rolled their eyes at on the radio yesterday and feeling that no matter what you did or said the people in that room would always want you. She remembered the colour of the dress she'd worn and the way Bailey's younger cousin, visiting from out of town, watched them from the top of the stairs until they coaxed him to come down and dance as well.

They sat until almost everyone else left, helped wrap up sandwiches and throw out sushi, the rice hard and brown from sitting out too long, slid stacks of creamy white envelopes into a small box that Bailey's parents would take home. Bailey's mother thanked them for coming and Laurel had to force herself to maintain eye contact. She and Catherine walked home afterward, silent most of the way. There did not seem to be any words to talk about what had happened, nor did it seem possible to not talk about it.

***

After the service, Laurel took a Tylenol and went to bed. She slept soundly and woke in the morning with a headache and a dull pain in her stomach. At work that night the pastry chef set out a plate of cupcakes for all the servers that were going to be starting school next week. There was a smooth, cold chocolate filling in the centre and piped buttermilk frosting on top. Laurel wrapped hers up in tinfoil and put it in the change room with her shoes and purse. Craig, one of the dishwashers, stood eating his over the sink, little black crumbs dotting the soap suds of the water. Craig was talking with one of the line cooks, whose mother was a nurse at the hospital.

"She said he came in and was like-" the cook let her eyes fall slack for a moment, "foaming at the mouth and shit."

Craig nodded encouragingly and shoved his index finger, wrinkled from the dish water, into the centre of the cupcake. A dollop of chocolate lay on the tip of his finger, staining his nail even after he'd licked it off.

"His dad was working and came out and saw him. They had to decide pretty much right away if they were going to harvest his organs 'cause I guess you only have like, an hour before they go bad." She paused in her story to remove a pan of bread warming in the oven. She fanned out four pieces of bread on a paper doilie'd plate, tucked thin slices of cheese into a wicker basket and banged the dessert bell. "Anyway. His dad called the mom and I guess once she showed up you could hear her screaming from the end of the hall."

Laurel was polishing glasses at the service station, a half flight of stairs down from the kitchen. She pressed the lever on the plastic

80

spray bottle, drops of vinegar and warm water tousling the base of the wine glass in her hand.

"That's sad," Craig said dumbly.

"Stupid," she corrected him and slammed on the dessert bell again. "Jesus, Laurel. I can see you right there." Laurel set her glass down, draped the green cloth on the table beside the bottle. Anger was a hot surge in her chest. Sharp words fought their way to her lips. Laurel swallowed them like bile. She took the plate and the basket and nudged the door into the dining room open with her hip.

When she came back into the kitchen, the line cook, Maura, was sitting on the metal countertop that connected to the walk-in freezer. She was writing down everything they would have to order from the farm for next week and drinking a beer. Laurel supposed she could have forgiven her had the conversation drifted elsewhere by the time she'd returned. Maura tilted her head backwards and lazily poured the beer into her mouth. She burped quietly. "Apparently they couldn't get the dad to stop doing-" she mimed chest compressions with her hands. "Like. He was brain dead. Jesus. Y'know?"

Laurel turned around. She felt braver than she sounded- her voice shook, and she held her hands to the side of her skirt to keep them still. "You're talking about a person." A surprised smile spread slowly across Maura's face. "Bailey, right?" Laurel asked.

Maura shrugged. "I don't know. My mom didn't tell me his name- doctor patient confidentiality."

Laurel laughed, short and loud. The sound scared her. "Right, because she really spared the details about everything else that happened."

"Man, I'm sorry. I didn't know you knew him, or I wouldn't have said anything. Were you fucking him or something?"

Laurel was crying. "No," she yelled. "No, I wasn't fucking him. He had a girlfriend. He's my friend."

"Laurel," Maura put her beer down. "I'm sorry. Honestly. I didn't know-"

"Just stop talking about him, okay?"

Maura nodded. She looked like she wanted to say more but thought better of it and went into the freezer to see how many shallots they needed.

***

Curtis was sitting at the breakfast bar, legs drawn up onto his chair, prodding half-heartedly at a stack of pancakes on his plate. She could hear, but not see, her father in the backyard chopping wood for the fire, could hear the heavy thud of the axe, the dry rustle of leaves. Her mother had gone out to collect the turkey from the butcher. It was the Saturday before Thanksgiving.

She'd taken the train home last night, a small blue duffle bag tucked under her seat and a few textbooks strewn across the fold down table of the train, their pages dog eared and margins overflowing with hastily scribbled notes. Maggie made lasagna and chocolate cake and Laurel had never imagined she could be so happy to spend an entire night lying on the worn leather couch in their basement watching baseball with her dad. The sheets on her bed were cool and smelled of lavender and she slept better that night than any since she'd left for school.

She told Curtis she was going to meet her friends and he nodded at her by way of farewell- he launched himself at her when she stepped off the train last night and spent the car ride home showing her new packs of trading cards he bought, talking about all the movies she'd missed, but retreated back to feigned indifference to her by the time the dinner dishes had been washed.

The leaves on the oak tree kitty corner from their house were bright orange, bitter yellow, dark red, the very essence of autumn. The air smelled crisp and clean. The children from the house across the street were playing in their front yard. They wore matching, unbuttoned raincoats and shrieked as a swirl of wind blew a pile of raked leaves at them.

Catherine and Addie were sitting at their table by the time Laurel got to the river. Catherine and Addie stood up and the three of them instantly had their arms intertwined around each other, foreheads pressed together, hands squeezing hands.

It was the first time she'd been home. Forrest had still gone out west, three weeks later than he and Bailey originally planned. He'd brought Bailey's ski goggles with him and sent them a photograph of the goggles on top of the dresser in his bedroom.

The first time Laurel spoke about Bailey at university was the third week of school, to her roommate who was kind and quiet and who brought Laurel tea just the way she liked it without being asked. The experience of trying to explain her friends to people who had never known them was bizarre and comforting and heartbreaking. "He sounds really special," her roommate said sincerely.

A single blue canoe floated on the water. It carried a father and two young children. The children's heads were barely visible above their puffy life vests. All afternoon, she waited for a sign about Bailey- she hadn't believed in god since she was thirteen, but a tiny part of her wanted to believe he was in something like heaven. Laurel was half expecting a red cardinal to swoop down or a cloud to take the shape of his initials as it passed above them. Instead, the sun warmed their backs and the laughter of the children in the canoe reverberated towards them as it carried across the calm water and branches on trees swayed when the wind came.

Ten

She was twenty-three years old and home for the first time in almost ten months. Home was home because she was born here, because over there was where she had her first kiss and because she could still remember all the names of her elementary school teachers; it could not be home anymore because she had to make herself small again to fit here, because three hours away in an apartment that her mother would have called "deplorably small" was her girlfriend and their cat, a string of Christmas lights and a wall papered with lists of things that the two of them were going to do together one day. "Find a recipe for really good Béarnaise sauce. Visit that ice hotel in Amsterdam. Make something that has never existed before."

She had made it as far as driving to her house and she could see the tree in the living room. For a moment, she remembered Christmas mornings past that all sort of blended together into a warm blur - wrapping paper strewn across the carpet and mugs of powdery hot chocolate and the flimsy paper crowns they wore at the dinner table.

She could still feel her mittened hand clasped in her father's gloved one as her led her up the icy steps of the church. She and her family were at service ever Sunday and she was always surprised by how many more people came for Christmas Eve mass. "These people are not true followers of God, Katherine," her dad would whisper in her ear as she sat perched on his knee, in the pew right at the front that was theirs every week. "Yes Daddy," she would try and steady her heart against these bad people. When she was very young, she loved to watch her father's sermons. She loved the way everybody listened to him. She loved that sometimes, if he was in the right mood, she could catch his eye and he would wink at her. Once after service she had asked her father if he *was* God. For a moment, anger flashed across his face, and then he laughed and laughed.

Katherine had turned the radio off in the car and she watched as her mother plugged in the lights of the tree and fiddled with the cards strung up on the wall. She couldn't go in, not yet anyway, and so instead she was in line at a coffee shop. It was the same one she went to every day in high school; by the time she was in Grade Eleven, the baristas all knew her by name. "It's Katherine," they would say with a smile, and often they'd have her drink ready before she'd even ordered it. Now, she didn't recognize anybody there and nobody recognized her. She couldn't decide if the anonymity was delicious or depressing.

The girl behind the counter called out, "Next" and it took Katherine a moment to realize she was speaking to her. The girl was probably sixteen, wearing purple eyeshadow and a thick gold necklace. "Do you know what you want?" she asked pointedly. "Um." The girl looked at Katherine expectantly. "I'll just get a medium latte." She called out "Next" before Katherine had finished paying.

Katherine moved to the end of the bar and watched as a middle-aged woman steamed a little pitcher of milk. The woman wiped the steam wand with a green cloth, poured the milk into a mug and then began steaming another pitcher. Katherine felt something move beside her and looked down to see a boy, no older than three. His hair was blonde, and he was resting his chin on top of the counter. "Woah," he said every time the woman restarted the process of steaming the milk.

The woman handed Katherine her latte. Though she ordered it to go, she went to a chair by the front window and sat down. The paper cup was warm against her hands and she held it until just before the moment when it would begin to hurt. She sat it down, cooled her hands on the leather of the chair, then picked it up again.

She remembered being eighteen, sitting on the back deck with her mother, Abigail. It was early June, a few days after her high school graduation. Katherine was digging her fingernails into the jean material of her shorts and promising herself that by the time she counted to ten she would release her fingernails and be honest with her mother.

"Patricia called this morning, sweetheart. She wants to know if you're planning on going back to camp."

Ten. "Um. I don't know, Mom. I thought you said I could be done after last summer?"

"You know how much it means to your dad." Her church, her father's church, had been running its summer camp since Katherine was three. She'd been going every season since, as a camper for ten years and a counsellor for four more. At some point between those fourteen summers, church camp became another bullet point on the list of things Katherine was bad at. They played capture the flag and decorated flowerpots with paper crosses and doves. At the end of each session, they had a service with all the campers. For these services, her father wore jeans and a baseball cap. He said things like, "Jesus is actually not that different from you guys!" and, "The coolest thing about God is how much He loves us."

Katherine was thirteen and painting a mural on the side of the church garage at camp the first time she heard the word dyke, muttered under the breath of some boy who was cleaning his paintbrush beside her. At home that night, Katherine and her father ate ham sandwiches on the picnic table where she and Abigail now sat. She remembered the sun was warm on her bare legs and her father let her have two bowls of mint chocolate chip ice cream after supper. "Today was so great, Katie Cat."

Nine. Eight. She closed her eyes; she was eleven years old, sitting cross legged on her bedroom floor with her best friend

Valerie, their lips pressed together, she was fifteen and in the cafeteria with her friends, scrambling to make up the names of boys she knew she was meant to like, she opened her eyes.

Seven. Her mother nudged Katherine in a way that was meant to be playful. "Patricia said they've had a lot of boys sign up. Maybe a little summer romance before you go to school?" Abigail's eyes were equal parts bright with the joyous prospect of her only daughter finding a nice boy to fool around with for the next two months and with the deep-seated anxiety that this would never be the life her daughter would choose.

Six. Five. It always confused her how people could have so many contradictions within themselves, like a riddle her grandfather once wrote on the inside of a birthday card for her; "I went to the pictures tomorrow/I took a front seat at the back/I fell from the pit to the gallery/And broke a front bone in my back/." Her parents were the kindest people she had ever known. Four days of the week, her mother made dinner for the widowed man who lived in the apartment building at the end of their street. Her father mentored a group of foster kids after school on Tuesdays and sometimes on the weekend they'd come over and have pizza and play Katherine's old Mario Kart games. In the front hall of the house they had a wooden plaque that read *Love Lives Here.* And yet they could be so hard and relentlessly unforgiving in a way that frightened her. They said cruel things but disguised them in kind words and they loved everybody except for the people they absolutely hated.

Four. "Mom, I-"

"You could go on a few dates, at least. It doesn't have to be anything serious and that way you'll know what to expect at college... you won't end up making any mistakes. You're a good girl." Abigail smiled.

Three. Two. "I know you and Dad... I know that-"

Abigail reached out and pried Katherine's hand away from her thigh. She ran her fingers over the tips of her daughter's, the way she used to when Katherine was little. She was silently pleading with Katherine to keep everything the same. Katherine smiled and swallowed everything she wanted to say, and said instead, "One more summer might be okay." It was a balancing act, one she had been trying to maintain for as long as she could remember. It was the art of existing without ever existing fully.

Eight weeks later, Katherine would call her mother from her shoebox of a dorm room. She told Abigail, in the gentlest way she knew how, that she was not, and could never be, the kind of daughter her mother wanted. "I've known since I was eight," she said into the phone, eyes closed tightly even though she was two hundred kilometers away from home. "But you always wear dresses", was the first thing Abigail said. "Your father can never know", was the last.

Katherine's cell phone, tucked in the pocket of her coat, vibrated against her leg. The blonde boy was still standing at the counter. She could not remember what it felt like to be enchanted by the most ordinary things, though she could remember spending an entire afternoon in the backyard with her parents searching for four leaf clovers and so she knew at one time she might have been able to listen, over and over again, to the paper-tearing sound of foaming milk with the same intensity that he was.

Katherine thought about that girl sometimes, the girl who sat on her father's lap and hated an entire church full of people she knew nothing about, the girl who agreed to hide herself, so things could stay simple for her mother. She wondered if that girl would recognize the Katherine who held her girlfriend's hand in the mall, the Katherine who hadn't had a Thanksgiving at home in three years.

Her phone vibrated again, and Katherine promised herself that by the time she counted to ten she would stand up, get in her car and go home.

Yesterday's Child

I lost them simultaneously, though Helena would later say it was them who lost me. "But I was the one who left," I insisted. "Nobody tried to come after you. They allowed you to leave," Helena said. I would learn to be thankful for this.

Us girls had to stop going to school once we reached Grade Nine – after that, we did Home Education: finishing seams, weaning babies, dicing vegetables. From the other girls in Honour, through fragmented whispers and snatches of conversation, I also learned what it meant to give a blow job, who Michael Jackson was, what a comic book looked like.

Before that, we were permitted to attend public school, but forbidden from speaking to the other children. Father Martin told us that non-Children of Honour were devil-worshippers. "It is through no fault of their own," he spoke through a wireless microphone, thin lines of bubbly spit threatening to snap when he grew too exuberant, "that their parents have contaminated their pure souls with the evil of the world. It is not up to us to save them, though it is natural we may wish to."

My first memory is sitting on our living room floor while a girl sits on the couch behind me. My bony shoulder blades are in-between her knees and she is braiding my hair. She could be my sister, cousin, or fellow Child - the lines between all three seem blurred, especially now in memory. My mother and father are in the kitchen. They are laughing – my father's hands are tanned with being outside all day, he is telling my mother a story from his day. My mother's hair is clipped back, and her white apron is discoloured from knee-high dirty handprints, spilled broth, garden soil. There are children playing around them in the kitchen, children playing behind the couch, children playing outside. The first time I spoke about it to Helena, I said, "You'd be surprised how many things were great, there." She squeezed my hand and said, "That doesn't surprise me," even though I knew it did. It was little things like that which made me fall in love with her.

The Honourable Children – a group of men whose roots were thick and deep in our community – met nightly with Father Martin. My father was not an Honourable. We shared our homes with each other, and my Uncle Peter, with whom we lived for the entirety of my childhood, was a member. He left the house every evening after supper and my father used to stand at the front window and watch him go down the road. The rest of us had service four times a week. We packed into the church, our legs pressed together, babies on laps, small children in the aisles. Father Martin preached about a great number of things but his favourite topics were Judgement Day ("For those of us who have done right by the Lord, this is a day to be revered and celebrated."), the homosexuals ("Men and women who practice homosexuality will never inherit the Lord's Kingdom … we must pity but never condone these odious acts.") and the Outside World ("Those of you who came to live at Honour, who have chosen to renounce the ways of the rest of the world and raise your children as beings of the Lord, are blessed.").

Every Sunday, Father Martin chose members from Honour who needed Reminding. If a person was chosen more than three times in a year for a Reminder, they were exiled. There were certain things which necessitated instant exile: drinking, dating somebody without seeking Father's permission, owning a television. Sundays with no Reminders were seldom, but glorious. On these days, Father Martin would tell us how proud he was. We would eat egg salad sandwiches in the hall after and at home there would be small treats for the children. I was picked for Reminder twice in my seventeen years at Honour. The first time, I was nine years old. I beat a boy from Honour for the top mark in Math for the Grade Four class. The boy's name was Jackson. I stood in front of our community; a baby waved at me from the lap of her mother, and Father berated me. "Girls who do not know their place are not good for Honour. Girls become women. Women are wives and mothers. 'Wives, submit to your own husbands, as to the Lord.'. Girls who think themselves superior to boys grow up to be dirty, disobedient, devils." Even as the shame washed over me, I remember noting Father Martin's use of alliteration. When we got home from service, my father laid me across his lap and whipped my backside with the bottom of his shoe. Most fathers would have used a belt. My mother cried while he was doing it and pressed a peppermint candy into my hand after.

There was happiness, too; one weekend in the summer, we gathered outside the church. Foil trays filled with shaving cream lay on the grass and small bottles of food colouring stood next to the trays. We poured the food colouring into the cream and stirred the dye in with popsicle sticks. We pressed cut pieces of paper into the mixture and scraped the excess foam back into its tray. Swirls of blue and pink and green danced across the paper. At home that night, we hung them up on our bedroom windows. I shared a room with three of my sisters, and Uncle Peter's two daughters. Even at that age, I knew I was different from the other girls. I lay in bed across from Uncle Peter's eldest girl, the moonlight pale and creamy on her cheek, and imagined what it would be like to kiss her.

I had been kissed by boys in Honour. One evening, behind the church, a boy cupped my breasts with his clammy hands. His erection pressed into my hipbone. In many ways, we were no different from the teenagers who kissed covertly in the backseats of cars while their parents thought they were at the movies.

My second Reminder occurred when I was sixteen. We kept journals, all of us. It was required, but I enjoyed the writing. The journal writing was reminiscent of school days, and I had loved school: copying from the blackboard, worksheets littered with sums. The journals were meant to be a vessel through which we could communicate to the Lord. We were encouraged to confess our sins, to speak on the sins of others, to express our devotion. I attempted to convey piety in my journal but was not usually successful. As a child, I was gifted at being everything others wished me to be. I was often chosen by my school teachers to explain problems to those who didn't understand them; at Honour, I understood how to be meek and obliging, and my mother would half-heartedly implore my siblings to, "be more like Polly." My journal entries were the place where I felt I could be most myself; we were assured that they were private, and so I allowed myself to write freely.

I'm still not sure who told Father Martin: it may have been on the grounds of suspicion (we'd had Games Day that previous weekend and the girls all changed into the leggings and knitted sweaters that were our sporting clothes together, and maybe my eyes had wandered unconsciously to the curve of a spine, the dip of clavicle) or perhaps it was a lucky, spiteful guess.

That Sunday, Father Martin announced those who would be receiving a Reminder: myself and a boy named Gilbert. Gilbert went first. He had spoken to a woman that came to report on Honour. These people came sometimes from the Outside World – people with cameras hung around their necks and notebooks clasped in their hands. "What are you doing here? When do you expect Judgment Day? Don't you see what this is?" Unless their presence was expressly approved by Father Martin, we were to pretend they didn't exist. I don't know if it was because of what was to come, but Father Martin was unusually benevolent when he spoke to Gilbert. "It is normal to feel curious," he said, hand heavy on Gilbert's shoulder, "and sometimes we are led astray from the Lord's desires. We must resolve to do better next time, to shield Honour from those whose own curiosity is impure and greedy." Gilbert returned to his seat, cheeks inflamed.

A few days ago, I'd been in the kitchen with the younger girls. It was their first year of Home Education, and I was teaching them

94

how to make a pasta sauce. Without thinking, I'd used too much salt. The sauce had to be thrown out. Wasting resources was an offence, though not always a serious one. I suspected maybe there had been no other mistakes committed that week and so, in a state of agitation, Father had chosen to make an example of Gilbert and me.

He pulled from his pockets a brown notebook and began to read. "'I know it's wrong, but I can't stop thinking about the way Florence laughs when I make a joke. Some days I feel all I do is try to think of ways to make her laugh. At school, I remember there was a boy who had two mothers. Sometimes they came together to pick him up and held hands. I think it might not be so bad.'" Father closed the notebook, using his finger as a placeholder. He raised the notebook so that everybody could see it. His breath was warm on the back of my neck.

"If I told you that these words came from the young woman who stands before me, I have no doubt many of you would question me. Polly has demonstrated outward devotion to Honour. And yet, she has deceived us. These words were found in Polly's journal. They have caused me a great deal of anguish; Polly is a child of Honour. She has allowed herself to be led astray, she has invited the devil to infiltrate her spirit. I fear deeply for Polly, as I'm sure you all do. In most cases, there would be no question as to my course of action. Polly would be thrown out of Honour. However, I'm sure we can all agree that Polly is an invaluable member of our community. Last evening, at an Honourable meeting, we spoke of this problem."

I thought of my Uncle Peter that previous evening, shrugging himself into his coat, kissing my Aunt Tabitha goodbye, my father watching him disappear into the evening, walking to the church. My eyes found my mother's.

"We believe if Polly is willing to renounce the devil and attend remorse sessions with myself, we can find it in our hearts to allow her to stay at Honour. Polly is sick, and if she wishes, we will do our best to heal her. Polly, I invite you to spend the rest of today reflecting. It is up to you to decide the kind of person you wish to be."

I left service early and walked home by myself; depending on the severity of a Reminder, we were allowed to do this. I sat on the front porch of our house and waited for my family to return. Our house was at the top of a small hill, and I heard them before I saw them. My siblings and Uncle Peter's children scattered as they walked, going to play by the pond, going to play inside. The older girls would be at church still, preparing for the next night's Honourable meeting. My father walked into the house without looking at me. My mother stood, for a moment, beside me.

A symphony of words fought their way to my mouth. In a muffled, restrained voice, I heard my father call for my mother. She disappeared inside. I went in shortly after. I could hear my parents muted voices in the living room. I hovered near the door and then went upstairs to the bedroom.

I sat heavily on the side of my bed. I stretched my hand out, gathering the fabric of the duvet in-between my fingers. Something crinkled beneath my pillow as I shimmied the duvet fabric: a peppermint candy, tucked under the bedcover. I wondered how long my mother had known.

My door opened. "Polly," my mother's eyes were swollen from crying.

I didn't know how scared I was until I saw her. "What do I do?"

She sat beside me on the bed. She seemed ten years older than she had before service. Once, when I was small, I got the stomach flu and was sick throughout the night. My mother stayed beside me. I woke in the early morning to her running her fingers through my hair. She gave me a glass of ginger ale to drink and sang to me.

My mother's hand went to my back. She closed her eyes. "This place isn't good for you, baby." If Father Martin ever heard my mother say that, she would be sent away. My entire family would be shamed. "You deserve to be happy."

In her permission for me to leave, I became desperate to stay. "Dad can't … he understands. He loves you," she said. She was quiet, I was crying. I felt like I would be sick.

I left later that day, in the back of a blue pick-up truck. It came right to my house. Most of Honour encircled the truck. They held hands and prayed. My father stood on the porch, his back turned to me. His shoulders were moving, and I wondered whether he was crying or praying, or both. He was holding my baby brother. My mother reached up from the prayer circle and quickly squeezed my hand.

I met Helena three weeks later in a girl's hostel in the city. I had just been hired at a grocery store. I had been given my first haircut. I often woke in the night to find I'd been crying in my sleep. I missed my family. I missed Honour. I thought of my mother, often. I wondered if my sister had become pregnant.

I live now with Helena on the fourth storey of a walk-up in the city. We have a dog and plants. We own a television and we go out dancing. I don't know if I'll ever feel fully adjusted, if I'll ever be able to walk past a church without feeling a deep-rooted sense of terror and shame. Sometimes I wonder whether things weren't simpler and better at Honour. We have a hand-stitched blanket on our bed; we hold hands on the street. We keep a bowl of peppermint candies on a table in the front hall.

Suitcase Heart

I met Steven in the middle of February. I read somewhere once that February is the most depressing month of the year, but it's also the shortest, so if you're going to have a miserable month then you might as well schedule it for February. I remember the winter I was eight and on Valentine's Day it snowed three feet overnight. All the kids that showed up to school sat in a small circle in the gym and exchanged cards and candy. We were drawing love hearts on the chalkboard and one of the teachers told us that the hearts inside our chests looked different than those. There are so many funny things you believe when you're a child and maybe you'd go on just sort of believing them forever if nobody bothered to tell you otherwise.

My family always jokes that a twenty-minute trip to the grocery store turns into an hour if you're with my mother because she can't pass a turnip without stopping to talk to it. She has smoked cigarettes for as long as I can remember, and my little brother and I sometimes tag along when she goes to the corner store to buy more. She smokes them standing in our kitchen, blowing the smoke through the little diamond holes of the screen door. She only ever smokes half a cigarette at a time. I think maybe it makes her feel better if she smokes six half cigarettes in an hour instead of three whole ones in thirty minutes. She knows the family who owns the corner store where she buys her cigarettes. She knows that their daughter goes to school in Toronto and wants to be a lawyer and comes home on weekends to work at the store. She knows that their son plays rugby and has a girlfriend who loves dogs and that on Sundays after church he helps his grandmother with her English.

People are drawn to my mother like magpies to silver coins and while I'm not sure I'll ever be as confident as she is, I think I've inherited a little part of that part of her. Once I was waiting at a train station and the woman beside me started talking to me. I learned that she'd been born in Minnesota but moved to New Jersey after her husband died and that she and her sister had been close when they were teenagers but after their mother died they sort of stopped talking and that when she was a girl her favourite thing to eat was banana upside down cake.

I was in-between everything that February. I was taking a break from university. All my friends were off at school and the town I had grown up in, every inch so familiar it used to feel like an extension of my home, felt cold and closed off to me now. Since I was nineteen years old, coming home had been an event, brackets that included eating Thanksgiving dinner on the deck, my mother saving the porcelain snowman for me to put on the tree, my little brother's birthday, a summer job, always the eventual return back to school. Everyone kept telling me I was brave for leaving university, but all I felt was defeat, slathered thick and heavy on my skin. I'd taken to going to this coffee shop downtown, mostly for something to do and that day it was snowing outside, and I was sitting writing, when the man at the table beside me started talking to me.

"Are you from here?" was the first thing he asked me. Here is a small town in southwestern Ontario. Here is firefighters lining the field by our house with plastic tarp after the first big snowfall, flooding the tarp and letting it freeze and kids coming in hordes on Saturday mornings to play hockey. Here is November 1st, road blocks on either end of the street by the river, people staggering their pumpkins single file by the curb and when it gets dark, the road lights up with the shadows of ghosts and cats and Jack-O-Lantern smiles. Last year, the Globe and Mail called us the most multicultural small town in Canada but in my graduating class of two hundred students, there was a hundred and ninety-four white kids and in the parking lot after school, white boys rolled down the dusty windows of their trucks and sang racial slurs like they had any right to the words. I was twenty-one years old and I loved 'here' but I loved it a lot more when I was away, and it was mostly a there.

"Yeah. Are you?"

He shook his head. "Born in North Bay. I'm an actor. My name is Steven."

"My name is Cree." I said. His hair was greying and curly. He had a small nose and the tip of it pointed up a little and his eyes were big and kept flitting around the coffee shop.

"That's beautiful. Is there a story there?"

"My parents found it in a newspaper four years before I was born and fell in love with it. They decided if they ever had a daughter, they'd call her Cree. They both thought I was a boy the whole time my mom was pregnant. They sang 'Take Me Out to the Ball Game' to me a lot."

He smiled. "What do you do?"

People had been asking me this question since I finished high-school, and people that knew I had come home from school asked me a variation of it now- what are you going to do? I thought about lying, about saying I was home for the weekend, about telling him I was in law school, but instead I sort of laughed and said, "Nothing, right now. I was at university in Toronto. I'm not, right now."

He nodded. "What do you want to be?"

"A writer." My words were quiet. For so many years, I volunteered this information as a definitive statement- I am going to be a writer. My dad taught me to read when I was five years old. I wrote my first story when I was six; I was a shy, uncertain child and books were where I never felt out of place. As soon as I was old enough to learn I could create worlds like the ones I'd been inhabiting, pink reading lamp lit up under my butterfly sheets well after my mother had turned off the light in the hall, I knew it was what I wanted to do for the rest of my life. I went to university with the vague idea that I would spend four years reading the same kind of books I'd loved my whole life, that I would be as smart as I'd been in my high school English class of twenty-eight kids, that I would graduate and maybe move to New York and get a job at a restaurant and start writing. The anxiety that had occasionally danced through my life when I was younger found a permanent home inside of me at university. I learned that, at least within the context of my school, I was underwhelmingly average and unimportant. I learned to believe that loving to read and wanting to write were not nearly enough. At the risk of sounding like a clinically misunderstood teenager, I learned to believe that I was not nearly enough.

He smiled. "What's your name, again? I'm sorry- I was diagnosed a few months ago with dementia. I'm doing pretty well, but names sometimes run away from me."

"It's okay. It's Cree. I'm sorry to hear that." I wasn't sure what to say. One grandparent on either side of my family had dementia. My mother's mother called us jubilantly last week to tell us that the nurse had made a mistake and she did not, in fact, have dementia. My grandfather came on the phone after to assure us that the nurse never said this, but that my grandmother was happier than she'd been in weeks and that they were going to have dinner at my uncle's restaurant to celebrate. My father's father was in a Home and he could usually remember his wife and sometimes his children. He loved pushing his dentures out of his mouth with his tongue when he thought nobody was looking and he'd laugh and laugh.

He smiled. "Don't be sorry. I don't feel any different- if that's okay. I can still do the dishes and come here. I know eventually I won't be able to do those things, but I've had a blessed life. There's nothing I haven't done that I wished I had. When I was a boy, I used to pray that I'd become an actor, and my dream came true. If writing is what you want, you've got to go for it. Go after the colours. Talk to yourself- if something you're doing isn't working, figure out why and change it. There will be lots of rejection and hard times, but if it's what you love then you have to do it."

Most of my friends have souls that belong to the arts. I live in a town whose one distinguishing feature from every other industrial factory town in Ontario is our theatre. With very few exceptions, the towns surrounding mine are all the same. They are filled with people who are mostly white and who vote mostly Conservative. The outskirts of these towns are littered with factories and the factories are mostly filled with sleepy men and women who stand for ten hours assembling car parts and come home hoping that they are building a future for their children that will be different from their own present. Our town has those things, too. When I was young, my father worked at the plant adjacent to the soccer field and if his lunch break aligned, he used to cross the street and watch me pick dandelions behind the goalpost while my team played. But we also have the theatre- we were a railway town before we were a theatre town, and then they closed down most of the passenger routes and we were an in-between town. A well-intentioned journalist believed that what we needed was a festival of Shakespearean theatre. The city council gave him a grant of $125 to go to New York City for artistic advice. That fall, a canvas tent was pitched on the field across from the river, a concrete amphitheater built the following summer. We've been a theatre town for 65 years.

There are endless platitudes to describe the way good theatre makes me feel and all of them make me think of a child's fist clutching at sand and the harder they try to show off the sand the quicker it falls in-between their fingers until they're left trying to explain something that nobody can even see. It is a space somewhere between dreaming and floating, and my peripheral vision goes a little hazy, like nothing that's existing outside the realm of the stage matters. It is the same feeling I get when I'm writing, and it comes in a crashing wave, enveloping my entire body.

I felt the wetness of my tears before I even knew I was crying. I had spent the better part of my last three years fighting and I felt like leaving university was a white flag hanging meekly from my front porch. Everything I thought I should, could and would become turned out to be wrong and perhaps those are the self-concerned words of a young woman who doesn't have the ability to understand that she isn't the only person who has ever felt this way, but I no longer knew where or how I should exist.

Steven reached across the table and put his hand on my elbow. It should have felt embarrassing or maybe even invasive, but I was grateful. "I'll get going," he said. "Wife gets nervous if I'm gone for too long. I'll see you again, Cree." He carried his cup and saucer to the counter, tugged his scarf tight around his neck and then was gone.

It's early spring now and I'm sitting in the same coffee shop, at the same table. It's a Saturday morning and it's cool for May, but the sun is warm and soon it will be summer. I've just finished the last of ten short stories that form the book I'm writing. It is called *Suitcase Heart*. The stories are made up of people and places from my own life, some of them truer than others. This is the only one that is entirely non-fiction. I haven't seen Steven since, but I think of him often.

Made in the USA
Middletown, DE
19 November 2018